I can't help but wonder how did I get here? I very moment? I'm so afraid I can't move.

I want to say something, anything but I'm te thing.

All I wanted was to be happy and to live my li.. ... ., knees, I don't think that either is possible.

How did I get here? How did I wind up at this very moment? Maybe I should start at the beginning.

My name is June Wynter, but people know me as Paige Anderson. I've always liked the name Paige and since my dad's name is Andy I decided to go with the synonym of Paige Anderson.

I was born in the city of Sparks, Nevada and raised by my single dad, Andy Wynter. My dad is a handsome, tall mountain of a man, a former Marine who settled with my mom and the true love of his life, Jesenia Mendez.

Two foster kids with no family to call their own, met, fell in love, married and began to start a family. That's the story my dad told me.

I never met my mother. I don't know what her voice would sound like or whether we would have been close. She died while giving birth to me, leaving my dad alone with an infant to care for.

With no one to rely on and a traditional job out of reach for a single dad, he became a self-employed handyman. Money was always an issue but he somehow managed. I never went to bed hungry and always had clothes on my back.

When I was ten, my dad finally saved up enough money to move us out of our tiny one-room apartment and into a tiny two-bedroom apartment.

I remember how happy I was that my dad, for as hard as he worked, could finally have a bedroom of his own instead of sleeping on the couch night after night.

I was introverted and a sad kid. I felt awkward around others. It didn't help that I was pretty and developed earlier than most girls. The boys always paid attention to me, but the girls did their best to act as if I didn't exist as bad as I wanted them to.

I had always known I was different, from my earliest childhood memories. As I became older it didn't help my awkwardness toward those of the same sex as I knew that I looked at them the way boys did. As the boys wanted the girls to see them that's how I wanted to be seen by them as well. I tried my best to fight the feelings that I had but it was a daily struggle.

I tried to convince myself, fight with myself and change the way I felt but I couldn't. Being so young I didn't understand what it was I was feeling and why I struggled so much. I remained an introverted kid until I met, Brenda Hastings.

When my dad moved us, it meant attending school in a different school zone When I met Brenda, things started to change for me. She immediately accepted me and introduced me to all her friends. She was outgoing, friendly sweet and sincere.

Truth be told I don't know why but I felt comfortable around her immediately. She knew I was a bit odd, but it didn't stop her from going above and beyond to get me out of my shell. We were thick as thieves and spent almost every waking second with each other. She was my best friend and I couldn't have imagined life without her. That was until I had to.

Midway through our freshman year of high school, she told me her dad was moving her and her mom to Seattle for his job. I was devastated!

As soon as she moved to Seattle my entire world changed. I soon discovered that I wasn't so much liked as I was tolerated by the girls at school. None of those girls were my friends, they were Brenda's friends. They were friendly with me because of Brenda and now that she was gone, they no longer felt obligated to be friendly toward me, so they weren't any longer.

This memory is as vivid today as it was the day it happened. It was the first day of school after winter break and Brenda had moved already. As I always did, I went to my usual table with my lunch in hand. As soon as I sat down, everyone and I mean everyone, rose from their seats and went to another table.

I could hear them talking about me.

"She thinks she's so much better than everyone else," Deborah said as Tiffany laughed out loud and said, "Model looks but a brain the size of a pea. Must be terrible to be so pretty but so poor at the same time."

Anna said, "I heard she's messing around with Andrew Chase." It seemed as the entire lunchroom heard every word that was said about me and agreed.

I felt like all eyes were on me, especially when Flora yelled out, "I heard she's also messing around with Sammy Knight! Makes sense, I mean isn't that what sluts do?! Fuck as many guys as possible!"

I couldn't take anymore. I was distraught. I ran out of the lunchroom and into the bathroom. I locked myself in a stall and cried my eyes out. I somehow managed to get through the rest of the day.

When I told Brenda about what was now happening at school all she said was, "I'm sorry I'm not there anymore to protect you."

I felt she should have told me but I kind of realized why she didn't. I was in Nevada and she was in Washington state, but we talked every day. All that changed the day I confided in her that I thought I may be gay.

I would tell you exactly how the conversation came to be, what I said and what she said but I can't bring myself to do so. The memory is too painful. Long story short, the day I told Brenda that I might be gay was the last time we ever spoke.

Whenever I tried to call her, I would get her voicemail. When I tried to call her at home one of her parents would always say she was either out or in the shower. It didn't take me long to get the hint.

At school, the girls who tried to be friendly I viewed as backstabbers and every boy who was friendly toward me, I attributed to wanting to get into my pants because of the constant rumors. Brenda was supposed to be my best friend, but she turned her back on me just because I confided my feelings. Why should I bother getting to try and know people? All I wanted to do was to graduate and leave school forever.

I again became that introverted and awkward girl. I ate lunch by myself, trusted no one and barely spoke during the day. My days were always the same. Eat breakfast, go to school, eat lunch by myself, walk home from school and go home. I would do my homework and spend the day watching television or listening to music until my dad arrived home from whatever job he happened to be working on.

My dad knew something was wrong but no matter how many times he tried to talk to me I would simply say that I was fine and if something was wrong, I would tell him. Thinking back, I don't know if it would have mad a difference anyway.

This was my life until a couple of months into my junior year of high school. That's when Danielle White walked into my homeroom and into my life.

"Ladies and gentlemen and anyone I've offended by saying the words ladies and gentlemen please welcome Danielle White to our lovely school," Mr. Tiggs announced.

He looked to his right and said with a commanding voice, "Ms. White please introduce yourself and when I say please, I mean now."

"Seriously?!" I heard a girl's voice yell out as Mr. Tiggs replies, "Centerstage now!" She had a unique sound to her voice as in an accent that I wasn't familiar with.

As if time was running in slow motion, I watched the beautiful girl with dark blond hair and amazing light blue eyes stand front and center in the middle of homeroom.

She had on a tight red tee shirt that made it seem like her tits were about to pop out that barely covered her stomach. She wore a pair of baggy black shorts and white running shoes.

I can't help but laugh when I think back as I can picture her in the front of that room chomping on bubble gum as if it happened an hour ago.

Danielle, as she chomped on her gum, said, "I'm Danielle. I'm from Lansing Michigan, by way of strong island, New York. My dad fucked his secretary and although my mom was fucking her boss, I was given the opportunity to choose between the lesser of two evils when they both found out they were cheating on each other so I moved to this shit town with my mom because I can stand her a tad more than my asshole father. That's all folks" she said as she blew a giant bubble and Mr. Tiggs lost his mind.

"Ms. White, if you want detention on your first day at school it will be my pleasure!" he barked as the entire room became silent.

She laughed and replied, "That's less time that I have to spend at home so bring it on!" as Mr. Tiggs smiled and responded, "Forget detention, spend quality time with your mom."

She rolled her eyes and said, "I prefer detention" as Mr. Tiggs smiled and replied, "I know" as the bell ending homeroom sounded.

Out of the five classes I had prior to the lunch period Danielle had four of them with me. When it was time for the lunch period, I did my usual and sat at a table by myself and began to eat.

"Are you stalking me?" I heard Danielle say to me. I turned my head and looked at her as she stood behind me.

"No, I'm not stalking you" I replied with anxiety.

"I don't know. Four out of five classes together and now lunch period too? Seems like a stalker situation to me" she said with a comedic tone to her voice.

I didn't know what to say or how to respond. I guess she could tell I was uncomfortable, so she laughed and said, "I'm joking. By the way, I'm Danielle and you are?"

I just started at her momentarily and then again turned my head, so I was no longer looking at her. I expected that she would walk away but she didn't. Instead, she sat next to me and said, "When I introduced myself that was your cue to introduce yourself to me."

"I'm June" I replied as the girls who I once thought were my friends, Deborah, Tiffany, Flora, and Jessica walked past our table and stared at us both with venom.

"Look the new girl is having lunch with the loser," Jessica said as Tiffany said, "Hey loser" to me as I put my head down and gazed at the table.

"What makes her a loser?!" Danielle snapped which took them all by surprise.

Flora began to laugh and replied, "She's poor and no one likes her because she's a slut who thinks she's better than everyone because of the way she looks. Anyway, you should have lunch with us. You don't want to be seen hanging around with her."

"I'm good where I'm at!" Danielle seethed.

"Guess that makes you a loser to" Deborah laughed.

Danielle laughed in reply and said, "I'd rather be a loser than ever hang out with any of you, cunts!"

"What did you just call us?" Flora asked with shock.

"I called you all cunts!" Danielle replied as she rose from her seat and stood with her arms at her sides with her fists clenched.

As they all walked away in shock and silence, I was so embarrassed I wished I were invisible. As I attempted to arise from my seat, Danielle placed her hand on my shoulder and pushed down on it.

She again took the seat next to me and said, "Who the fuck are those bitches?" I replied, "It doesn't matter."

"Yea, it matters. Why do they treat you like that? Better yet, why do you let them treat you like that?" she asked with conviction.

"It's just the way it is. I don't care anyway. In two years, it will all be over" I said to her as she shook her head.

We had lunch together and I discovered that we also had last period class together. I don't know how it happened but as the days turned into weeks and the weeks into months, I found myself constantly hanging out with Danielle at school.

We always sat next to each other and always walked with each other to our classes. She and I were complete opposites. She was outgoing and confident. She was nice to whoever was nice to her. She made it a point to say hello to anyone and everyone as we walked through the school. It didn't take long for Danielle to become one of the more popular people in school.

It wasn't until a few months into the school year that I discovered how different we truly were. It was a Thursday after school as Danielle and I walked and talked. I didn't realize it until we were both standing outside the apartment building that she had walked me home.

"This is me. Guess I'll see you tomorrow" I said as she looked at me and said, "Seriously?"

"What?" I responded as she immediately replied, "You're not going to invite me in?"

"I'm sorry. Do you want to come inside?" I asked as she smiled and nodded her head.

I didn't want her to come inside. What was she going to think of my tiny, barely furnished apartment?

She didn't bat an eye when we walked inside. She didn't judge me at all, even when I told her that the reason, I never gave her my cell phone number was because I didn't have one, that I didn't have cable television or internet access.

"Party this Saturday night. Gary Franks parents are going out of town so he's throwing a kegger" she said to me.

"Have fun" I replied as she laughed and responded, "I will, and you will too."

"Why would I have fun?" I asked as she smirked and said, "You're coming with me."

"No, I'm not," I said as she replied, "Yeah, you are." Over and again we went back and forth until I finally relented and agreed.

It wasn't until lunch the next day that I confessed to Danielle that one of the major reasons I didn't want to go to the party was because I didn't have anything nice to wear.

"I can take care of that" she replied.

After school, we walked to her house and my jaw nearly hit the ground when we arrived.

Her home was luxurious! In-ground pool, hot tub and huge! Her bedroom was bigger than my entire apartment!

She excitedly went into her huge walk-in closet and came out with an outfit.

"I can't," I said with a low voice as she smirked and replied, "You can, and you will."

I can't explain it, but Danielle had a way of convincing me to do things that I wasn't all too comfortable with. She didn't force me or anything it was just the way she explained things made me see things her way often.

When my dad hurt his back, I felt obligated to help financially, so I looked around for a part-time job and lucked out in finding one at a local ice cream shop. It didn't pay much but something was better than nothing.

Danielle was becoming my new Brenda, but I was worried. It felt great to have a close friend once again but if I confessed to her the way I did to Brenda would Danielle react the same? The thought started way back in my head but was soon all I could think about.

I was afraid so I decided against saying anything to her until I felt obligated to. It was my birthday and after I arrived home from dinner with my dad I walked to Danielle's as she insisted that I come over that night.

"Happy birthday bitch!" she yelled out as I laughed and replied, "Thank you."

It was a small box but kind of heavy at the same time. I unwrapped the present to find a cell phone. I looked at the cell phone with shock and then looked at Danielle's beaming smile.

"Do you like it?" she asked as I looked at her and replied, "I can't accept this. It's too much."

"It's not too much. Besides now I can call you on your phone instead of calling your house over and again. We can also text. Welcome to the age of technology" she said with sarcasm.

"No, Danielle. I can't afford to pay for service" I confessed.

"You don't have to. It's on my plan" she said with a coy smile.

"Danielle…" I began to say as she laughed and said, "I'm so happy you like it. No need to thank me but your welcome" she said with a tinge of sarcasm.

I don't know why but I felt I needed to tell her.

"Danielle, I think I'm gay" I confessed with my heart pounding as I attempted to hand her back the present.

She pushed it back to me and asked, "Think or know?"

"Well, I'm pretty sure," I said with a pained look.

"You ever do anything sexually?" she asked with intrigue as I quickly shook my head.

"You want to though?" she asked with the same tone to her voice as I slowly nodded my head.

"Who?" she asked.

I let out an awkward laugh and answered, "I can't answer that."

"Yes, you can. C'mon, if you could with anyone right now, who would it be?" she asked with building excitement.

"Francesca" I confessed with embarrassment.

"Holy shit, your boss?" she laughed out and continued, "Nice choice, she's definitely a MILF."

"I should go. I understand if you don't want to be friends anymore" I said with a low tone to my voice.

She exploded! "Why the fuck wouldn't I want to be friends with you anymore? Because you're probably gay?! Is that what you think of me?!" she yelled out and then gazed at me with her chest quickly rising and falling.

The as if she were hit with something, she looked at me and asked, "Is this why you and Brenda stopped being friends?" as I nodded my head.

"June, I'm not Brenda. I don't know what kind of person would turn their back on a friend over their sexual orientation, but I promise that I'm not that person" she said as she gave me a tight hug.

"I'm sorry," I said to her with tears forming in my eyes as she responded by saying, "It's okay, I'm sorry for yelling at you."

That day I realized that Danielle was the only true friend I ever had in my life. True to her nature, she didn't judge me, she accepted me for who I was. I felt relieved and knew that Danielle was special.

I continued to go to school and work at the ice cream shop.

The best part of working at the ice cream shop was my boss, Francesca Milano. She was married, had two young sons and was in her late thirties. She had long black hair, dark black eyes, gigantic tits, a voluptuous tight ass and curves for days. She stood around five feet five inches and was the very definition of a MILF! Whenever I was around Francesca, I could feel nervousness engulf my body, especially since she had a habit of always touching me.

When she walked past me, she would always place her hands on my shoulders and give me kind of a few second shoulder massage. When we were working together behind the small counter, instead of asking me to move so she could get past me, she would instead press her body against my back. I remember enjoying the feeling of her huge breasts pressed against my back as she slid her chest across my back to get past me. If I didn't know any better, I could swear that she was flirting with me but I kind of felt as if it was all in my head.

I looked forward to spending time with her after closing on Saturday nights as I helped her balance the books for the week. Just me and her in her small office at the back of the shop.

"June, you've been doing a fantastic job and I don't know where I would be without you," she said to me with a smile as she sat behind her desk with me sitting in a chair directly across from her.

"Thank you so much" I replied with a smile.

"Are you happy here?" she asked.

"I couldn't be happier" I replied not realizing I was staring at her chest.

Francesca smiled at me in a way I hadn't seen before and asked, "May I ask you a question?"

"Of course," I replied.

"Your friend Danielle that visits from time to time. Is she your girlfriend?" she said with an unfamiliar tone to her voice.

I bit the bottom right corner of my lip as I was unsure how to answer. Was it that obvious that I was crushing on Danielle?

With my voice quivering, I looked at Francesca and replied, "Why would you think she's my girlfriend?"

"It's the way you look at her," she said to me and continued, "Am I getting too personal? I don't want to cross any lines."

I let out another nervous laugh and responded, "No it's fine, but she's not my girlfriend."

Francesca smiled at me and said, "You have a crush on her."

I was a bit embarrassed but replied, "I guess it would be safe to say that."

"So, you're..." Francesca began to say. I could tell she was unsure if she should say what she was about to say but I knew what she was going to say.

"Gay. I'm pretty sure I'm gay" I said drawing out my words.

"Pretty sure, but not positive?" she asked with a serious look on her face.

I didn't know what to say. I swallowed hard and sat in the chair in silence.

She arose from her chair behind her desk, walked around the desk and took a seat on her desk directly in front of me.

"May I ask you another question?" she asked as I nervously nodded my head.

She smiled at me and leaned in toward me. With her face inches away from mine she asked, "Do I make you nervous?"

I could feel my face become flush and with my voice quivering I confessed, "Yeah, a little bit."

"Why do I make you nervous?" she asked with a flirtatious tone to her voice.

I again sat in silence.

"Do you find me attractive?" she asked as my heart began to pound in my chest and my entire body felt warm.

I couldn't bring myself to say anything, so I just smiled awkwardly.

"Can you double check my work?" she asked as I replied, "Of course" as I arose from my seat and took a seat at Francesca's chair behind her desk. As I looked over the spreadsheet before me, Francesca walked around the desk as was now standing directly behind me.

As I continued to look at the spreadsheet, she placed her hands on my shoulders and began to rub them. The way she was rubbing my shoulders made me feel like my body was melting. I could feel the tension leaving my shoulders as she continued to rub them.

"There's no reason to be nervous around me June. I don't bite unless you want me to" she said in a seductive voice.

I didn't know how to respond so I ignored her statement and said, "The books look great" as she stopped rubbing my shoulders as I rose to my feet.

As I began to attempt to walk out from behind her desk, I was stopped dead in my tracks as Francesca placed her hands on my hips and pressed her body against my back.

That all too familiar feeling of her breasts pressed against my back and the feeling of her hands on my hips made my entire body feel as it was engulfed in flames.

"Your hair smells nice," she said as I swallowed hard and replied in a low tone of voice, "Thank you."

With her body now pressed even more tightly against mine, she removed her right hand from my hip, ran her fingers through my hair and pushed my hair aside, exposing my neck.

She gently kissed my neck which made me gasp.

"Do you want me to stop?" she gently whispered into my ear as she again gently kissed my neck as I replied in a low tone of voice, "No."

She licked my earlobe and then gently bit it as I felt her right hand slowly move underneath and then up my shirt.

When I felt her fingers run across my nipple my entire body shook as she giggled and said, "Someone isn't wearing a bra."

"I was running late and forgot to put one on" I explained through my panting breaths.

She giggled and then proceeded to move her hand across both my tits, side to side, making sure to touch my nipples in the process which were now rock hard.

She removed her right hand from underneath my shirt, but it was soon replaced by her left hand. She now moved her left hand across my tits and nipples as she had been doing with her right hand.

She started gently kissing my neck as she rubbed my nipples and tits as I felt her right hand move under the waistband of my sweatpants.

I felt her hand make its way underneath my panties as she gently touched my pussy. She slowly began to run her fingers across my clit.

The feeling of her lips on my neck, her left hand on my left tit and the fingers on her right hand gently moving across my clit made my knees week. I was so turned on I could barely stand it.

"You're so wet," she said as she played with my pussy as I managed to get the word, "Uh-huh," to come out of my mouth.

Suddenly she removed her left hand from underneath my shirt and her right hand from my pussy. She spun me around, so I was no facing her.

She gently kissed my lips and smiled. "Your lips are so soft," she said. She then placed the two fingers she had been playing with my pussy with and licked them.

She smiled at me with lust and took me by my right hand. She walked me around to the front of her desk, looked at me and said, "Sit" as I now sat on the front of her desk as she had been earlier.

She pulled my shirt over my head and placed it beside me on the desk. I was beyond nervous as I didn't know what she wanted or was going to do to me. I crossed my arms which now covered my breasts.

"Don't be nervous. I want to see," she said as I slowly uncrossed my arms exposing my tits to her.

She slowly moved her face toward my tits and proceeded to gently lick my each of my nipples which made me moan in pleasure.

She again gently kissed my lips and then inserted her tongue into my mouth. I felt her tongue with my own as I felt myself become even more excited.

She removed her tongue from my mouth and then got onto her knees. She untied my sneakers and removed them both. She placed her hands on the inside of my sweat pants as I raised my ass slightly off the desk using my arms for leverage as she slid my sweatpants off my legs.

She sat down in the chair that I had previously been sitting in and moved in the chair to the front of my legs. She gently pulled them apart.

She slid my panties to the side. I watched her head move slowly toward my pussy and then felt her tongue lick my pussy. As I watched her head in between my legs and her tongue caress my pussy I didn't want her to stop.

"You taste so good," she said with passion as I again slightly rose my ass off the desk as Francesca slid my panties off.

She gently opened my pussy lips and began to lick my pussy. Without thinking for a second, I pushed my pussy closer to her mouth and grabbed the back of her head with both my hands. I gently pushed her head into my pussy as I placed my legs over her shoulders.

"Oh God, that feels so good!" I exclaimed as the excitement in my voice made her more excited as she ate my pussy more passionately.

As she licked and sucked on my clit all I could think to myself was, "I can't believe this is happening!"

When she inserted a finger into my pussy and begin to move it in and out of me as she licked my clit all I felt was pure pleasure.

Her finger was moving in and out of me lightning speed as was her tongue across my clit. I began to breathe more and more heavily as it felt like my entire body was becoming pressurized.

"Fuck…uh…yes…oh…um…um…um…yeah..yes…yes…yes!" I screamed out as it felt like the pressure that had built in my body was released like lighting shooting out of me.

As I had a mind-blowing orgasm, my first orgasm, Francesca stopped licking me and gazed into my eyes as she continued to finger fuck me as I came.

She slowly removed her finger from inside of me and smiled. I looked at her and laughed as I placed my hands over my face in embarrassment.

Suddenly, Francesca looked at the time and yelled out, "Shit, I'm late!" as she jumped out of her seat and looked at me.

"Can you please lock up? I have to go right now!" as I nodded my head.

Francesca wiped my juices off her drenched faced with a small hand towel, threw it to the ground and quickly ran out of the office and out of the store.

I removed myself from the desk and quickly dressed. I locked up the store and began my walk home.

One would think I would be upset due to the way Francesca ran out on me, but I wasn't. It felt like I was floating on air. I had thought I was gay, was pretty sure I was gay, but I now knew the truth. Any doubt that I had over my sexuality was forever gone.

However, that night as I laid in bed after a long hot shower, I finally made a confession to myself. Francesca was mature and sexy, and I was content that my first sexual experience with a woman was with her but deep down inside I wished it was Danielle.

She was my best friend, my only friend. If I had a choice, I would choose not but I didn't have a choice. No matter how hard I tried to fight the attraction I couldn't.

How could I? Danielle was funny, sexy, smart, kind and treated me better than any person not named "Dad" had ever. I tried to convince myself that if I fought the feeling long enough it would go away.

Of course, the very next day I told Danielle what happened between Francesca and me. She had a look of amusement on her face the entire time. After I finished giving her the play by play, she looked at me and laughed as she said, "It sounds like a bad porno."

Danielle now knew what I now knew. I was a lesbian, but she didn't treat me any differently than she had before.

The next time I went to work, after Francesca and I shut down for the day, we went into her office. She could tell something was wrong when she looked at me from across her desk.

"Something on your mind?" she asked as I nodded my head.

"You're married with children, but you did what you did to me. I'm a bit confused" I confessed.

"I love my husband Michael, but he knows that he can't always give me what I need. Let's just say he's open to me spending time with others as long as I don't flaunt it" she explained.

She looked at me and said, "I'm sorry about what I did. I just couldn't help myself" she said as if she felt bad about the encounter.

"I wanted it to happen," I said with a smile which brought a smile to her face.

"I don't think it's a good idea for us to do anything further. I'm your employer" she said as I replied with a disappointed voice, "Okay, if that's what you want."

As bad as I tried to fight what I was feeling toward Danielle it felt like a losing battle. I was attracted to her and wanted her badly. I had thought if I fought my feelings long enough, they would go away but they only became stronger.

By that summer, as hard as I tried to act normally as possible around her, I knew I wasn't.

On a Saturday night, Danielle and I decided that we would have a sleepover at her house. It was a normal night, not unlike any other night we had hung out.

I was sitting on her bed when she looked at me and said, "I'm thirsty, are you?" as I nodded my head.

"I'll go get us something to drink," she said as she left me alone in her room.

I removed myself from her bed and paced around in her room. That's when I noticed something out of the corner of my eye. White thong panties, Danielle's white thong panties! They were sitting just outside her hamper as if she attempted to throw them in and missed without realizing.

I picked them up and held them in my right hand. As I was about to place them inside her hamper, I don't know what came over me.

Instead of placing them in the hamper as I initially planned, I raised the crotch of the panties to my face and then to my nose. I closed my eyes and inhaled through my nose deeply. I again inhaled through my nose deeply as the smell of her panties brought a smile to my face.

"So, what do you think?" I heard Danielle ask as I quickly opened my eyes to discover Danielle standing in front of me, holding two glasses of iced tea with ice in her hand.

Danielle had just walked in on me sniffing her panties! I was beyond embarrassed as I looked at Danielle who to my surprise was smiling.

"I'm so sorry. I think I'm going to go" I said with embarrassment as Danielle looked at me with amusement and said, "Don't be ridiculous."

She extended the glass toward me as I took hold of it with my left hand. She put her glass down on her dresser and took her panties from my hand.

"So, what do you think?" she again asked with amusement.

"I'm beyond embarrassed. I don't know why I did that" I said with my voice quivering.

Danielle looked at me and laughed. "Don't be embarrassed. There's nothing to be embarrassed about anyway. To be honest I'm flattered" she said.

"Flattered?" I asked with shock.

She smiled, grabbed her glass from the dresser, took a sip and put it back down.

"We're friends and friends can be honest with another which is what makes a friend a friend," she said as a matter of fact.

"Okay?" I replied not having a clue as to what she was getting at.

"The reason you smelled my panties is that you wanted to know what my pussy smells like. Now that you have an idea as to what my pussy smells like you probably want to know what it tastes like" she said with confidence.

I was mortified and didn't know what to say!

She giggled at the expression on my face as she said, "It's okay. Besides, I wouldn't have a problem with it anyway."

"You wouldn't have a problem with what?" I asked with shock and surprise.

She again giggled and said, "If you want to go down on me that's cool."

What did she just say?! I thought for a moment and asked, "You would be okay with me wanting to go down on you or are you okay with me going down on you?"

"If you want to go down on me it's not a problem. You can if you want to" she said with a smile as she nodded her head.

Was she fucking with me? I wasn't sure if she was or not!

"If I say I want to go down on you right now you would want me to?" I asked trying to figure out whether she was fucking with me or not.

She grabbed her glass took another sip and again placed the glass on her dresser.

"Yeah sure. If you want to go down on me" she said.

"Why?" I asked with my voice quivering.

She laughed and replied, "Remember I told you about my friend Jessica back in Lansing? Well, we kind of messed around. No sex or anything but just kissing. Before we could experiment any further, I moved."

"Are you saying you're into girls?" I asked with my eyes practically popping out of my head.

"I like guys but I'm really curious about girls. I guess you could say that I'm kind of thinking I might be bisexual" she said without hesitation.

"You want me to go down on you?" I asked with my heart racing.

"If you want to, sure go down on me…" she said and then appeared as if she was deep in thought.

"We should kiss first," she said with a smile as she walked to her bed and sat on the foot of it.

I nervously sat next to her and then looked at her as she looked at me.

She laughed and said, "What am I thinking?" as I felt deflated. She was fucking with me the entire time!

To my surprise, she got off the bed, walked to her bedroom door, closed it and then locked it. She walked back to me and sat in her previously vacated spot.

"Where were we?" she asked as I replied, "Kissing?"

She shrugged her shoulders, tilted her head and moved her head toward me as I did the same.

Within seconds we were sitting on her bed French kissing. We stopped kissing, looked at each other and laughed.

"That was nice," she said as I nodded my head in agreement.

"So, should I just take my pants and panties off or do you want me to be completely nude?" she asked.

"Whatever you're comfortable with" I replied with my voice cracking.

She got off the bed, unzipped her shorts, unbuttoned them and removed them. She then removed the black thong panties she had on.

I swallowed hard as I looked at a bottomless, hairless pussy, sexy Danielle.

"How do you want me? Should I sit on the edge of the bed or should I just lay down and spread my legs?" she asked without hesitation.

"Are you sure you want to do this? Are you even attracted to me?" I asked as I felt myself begin to sweat.

"Of course, I'm attracted to you. You have a great pair of tits and a voluptuous firm ass. The face of a goddess body of a demon. You're hot!" she said with a wink.

"Okay, good to know. I guess you should just lay down then" I replied.

She placed two pillows on top of one another at the head of her bed and laid down. She slightly bent her knees and spread her legs.

"I'm ready when you are," she said.

I was beyond nervous, but Danielle was calm, cool and collected.

"All you've ever done was kiss a girl?" I asked as she looked at me and rolled her eyes.

"I'm waiting to get eaten out if someone would cooperate," she said with a comical tone to her voice.

I sat on the foot of her bed and stared at her hairless, pink pussy.

"Should I just go right in?" I asked seeking her advice.

"Go right in," she said with a tinge of excitement present in her voice.

I quickly wrapped my hair in a bun and then placed myself in between her legs. Her pussy was no inches from my mouth.

I closed my eyes and stuck my tongue out as I felt my tongue touch her pussy. I again licked and then without knowing what was coming over me, I buried my face in her pussy.

As I licked her, I could feel my face becoming soaked in her juices. She placed her legs on my back and pressed them together as my head was now locked into her pussy with the inside of her thighs pressing against each side of my head.

She tasted amazing! She had a tart, almost tangy taste which had a hint of sweetness to it. I loved the taste of her!

I stopped eating her pussy and asked, "Am I doing okay?" as she pounded on the bed and looked at me in amazement.

"Yes, and don't stop!" she said through clenched teeth.

I happily began to eat her pussy once again. I was like a girl possessed. It was like I knew exactly what I was doing even though I didn't. I guess you could say I was a natural!

Danielle began to sway her hips into my face and then began to move her pussy up and down over and again.

I watched her from in between her legs as she removed a pillow from beneath her head and placed it over her face. I watched her push the pillow over her face, almost as if she was trying to smother herself.

She pumped her hips into my face quickly as I heard you muffled screams of pleasure. After three forceful thrusts into my face, her legs began to convulse as she stopped moving and went limp.

I stopped eating her pussy and removed my head from in between her legs as she removed the pillow from her face and looked at me.

She giggled and then laughed as I looked at her blushing face.

She called me to her with her index finger. I climbed on top of her and then we French kissed.

I could tell she enjoyed the taste of herself present in my mouth.

We stopped kissing as she looked at me and said, "That was fucking amazing."

"So, I did okay?" I asked as she smiled with content and replied, "More than okay. It was like you were inside my head."

She went underneath the covers as I joined her. We cuddled and talked for a while.

We both changed for bed and slept that night cuddling and kissing.

In the morning, right before I left, she looked at me and said, "You can do that to me anytime you want to" I smiled and replied, "Good to know."

I'd be lying if I didn't say I was worried that experimenting sexually with Danielle would hurt our friendship, but it didn't one bit. We still did the same things we had always done together except that from time to time I would get her off.

She knew she enjoyed having me eat her pussy, finger fuck her, lick and suck on her tits and sitting on my face but she wasn't one hundred percent sure that she wanted to do those same things to me.

"Maybe you're just a pillow princess," I said to her one day jokingly as she shrugged her shoulders and replied, "Maybe you're right."

It was a couple of months into my senior year of high school. Danielle and I were becoming more sexually active together. Come to think of it, she wanted me to get her off more and more which I happily went along with.

It was Saturday night if I remember correctly.

"Where's your dad?" Danielle asked.

"Bowling as usual" I quickly responded.

She but her bottom lip and said, "Your room, now!"

"Oh really?" I asked as she nodded her head and replied, "Really."

"What do you have in mind?" I asked with intrigue.

"Promise you won't think I'm a freak," she said as I shook my head and replied comically, "I can't promise unless I know what it is you have in mind."

"How about I surprise you instead," she said with a coy look.

"Maybe," I said with a wink.

The tone of her voice not only intrigued me but made me excited.

"Clothes off!" she commanded as soon as I closed my door behind me.

"You want to do something for me?" I asked with passion in my voice.

"Yeah," she said with a nod and a smile.

"I need a quick shower" I confessed as she replied, "Great, come back nude."

As I showered my mind wandered with thoughts of what Danielle had in mind. I finished my shower, wrapped myself in a towel and quickly reentered my bedroom.

To my surprise, Danielle was fully dressed.

"I've been a very selfish girl," she said as I looked at her.

"Tonight, it's all about you. Well, making you feel good and me trying out a few things" she said comically.

"Game on," I said as she smiled and removed my towel.

She kissed me and then began to play with both my nipples in a circular motion with her finger which drove me insane.

"Lay down" she commanded as I laid down in my bed.

She sat at the foot of my bed, raised my leg in the air and proceeded to lick in between my toes and suck on my big toe.

"That tickles!" I yelled out with laughter as she removed my big toe from her mouth and placed my leg back on the bed.

She climbed on top of me and began to lick and suck on my nipples as I moaned with delight. She placed her right hand in between my legs and began to play with my pussy.

As she played with my pussy and clit, she kissed me passionately. I was completely turned on.

"I want you on all fours" she commanded as I laughed out and said, "Yes, ma'am."

I was now on my bed with my arms straight down to my side with both my knees on my bed.

She sat down with her legs beneath my body with her face inches away from my pussy. I could feel her warm breath on my pussy as she breathed.

"That feels so good," I said as Danielle licked my pussy from behind.

I was enjoying the feeling until I felt a bit weird for a moment. She was licking my pussy in an up and down motion when I felt her tongue brush up and down my asshole.

It felt good but odd at the same time. I thought that she maybe accidentally licked my asshole until she did it again and again. Before I knew what was happening, I felt her tongue enter my tight ass and begin to wiggle inside of me.

I wasn't sure if I liked it or not until I felt her begin to play with my clit. The feeling of her tongue inside of my ass, while she played with my clit, felt amazing.

"Tongue fuck my ass!" I exclaimed as Danielle begin to move her tongue in and out of my asshole as she continued to play with my clit.

A few seconds ago, I was unsure if I liked having my ass eaten but here, I was now was begging for Danielle not to stop.

As I orgasmed, I felt my asshole expand and contract around Danielle's tongue with each exhale of pleasure.

"What the fuck did you just do to me?" I asked as I sat on my bed panting.

She laughed and said, "I saw that in a lesbian porno, and I knew I wanted to try. What do you think?"

I looked at her with lust and responded, "I can tell you, but I rather show you!" with lust.

I quickly pulled off Danielle's short and panties and pushed her into position. As she had done to me, I now did to her.

The taste of ass is kind of unique. The best I can describe it is like pennies at the bottom of a beer glass. All I knew was that I discovered that I enjoyed eating a girl's asshole that night especially when I felt her asshole expand and contract on my tongue.

Thankfully Danielle and I stopped messing and got dressed a mere two minutes before my dad came home.

It's hard to explain but it was like Danielle and I had this unbreakable bond. A bond I never experienced with another person. No matter what we did sexually with each other our friendship never changed. No questions, no jealousy just complete and total friendship. I don't think that most people would be capable of having such a relationship, but we did.

It wasn't until after winter break of our senior years of high school when I felt that my feelings toward Danielle were more than what a person should feel for a person who was only a friend. This was especially true when she told me she would be going to college in New York. The thought of not having her in my life shook me to my core.

"June, what's wrong?" Danielle asked.

"Nothing is wrong" I quickly answered.

"I know you well enough to know when something is wrong. Tell me what's wrong" she said to me with sincerity.

"In eight months, you'll be leaving for New York" I replied.

"I know but I wanted to talk to you about something" she smirked.

"What would that be?" I asked.

"Come with me," she said with an ear to ear smile.

"I can't afford to go to college at Columbia and even if I did, I don't have the grades to get in," I said to her.

"So, go a city or state university" she responded.

"Even with student loans, my dad can't afford it. I would be an out of state student and with room and board tuition is still close to thirty grand a year" I replied.

"Fine, forget Columbia. I'll go to college here in Nevada" she said with seriousness.

Attending college at Columbia was her dream and she wanted to go back to New York in the worst way. She had been living in Lansing for less than a year before her parents separated, and she was relocated to Sparks. She had family and friends in New York that she missed terribly. How could I allow her to kill her dream and continue to miss all the people that meant so much to her?

"No, I couldn't let you do that," I said to her.

"Let me? I can do what I want. If I want to go to college in Nevada, then that's what I'm going to do" she said with raised eyebrows.

"Why would you want to do that?" I asked in a low voice.

Without hesitation, she replied, "You."

"What about me?" I asked with tears forming in my eyes.

"You June, you!" she yelled out.

"Danielle, stop, please. I don't want to argue about this again" I pleaded.

"I don't get it! What's wrong with us holding hands in public. What's wrong with me kissing you in public. Why are you so afraid of what people think?!" she yelled.

"You don't know what it's been like for me, you have no clue. I just want to graduate from high school and never see these people again. I'm not like you. I'm not as strong as you and I can't go back to being treated the way I was before and after Beth and before you came into my life. I just can't" I cried out.

"I'm sorry," she said as she hugged me tightly.

Danielle didn't have a choice at the end of the day over attending college in New York at Columbia. Her parents told her if she didn't go to Columbia as planned then they wouldn't pay for her tuition. We spent as much time together as possible both knowing full well that our time together would come to an end.

A week after my birthday and two days before graduation I waited for my dad to arrive at home as I always did but on this day he wouldn't return. The next time I saw my father was to identify his remains. He suffered a heart attack working on a house without the owner's presence. By the time the owners of the home arrived back from work he had already suffered a massive heart attack and had been deceased for hours. I buried him at a national veterans' cemetery in Nevada.

Had it not been for Danielle I wouldn't have attended our graduation ceremony. It was surreal. All those people who treated me like crap for all those years now offered me their condolences and told me how sorry they were. It made me sick to my stomach.

When Francesca's lease on the ice cream shop expired, she was forced out of business when the landlord wanted double the rent that she had been paying.

I was now alone and on my own with no income. My entire life felt like a nightmare that had come true. My dad left me everything he had. A couple of thousand dollars and his old rusted pickup truck.

Danielle did her best to get me out of the apartment and to try and get me out of my depression. Some days were better than others but not before long it was time for Danielle to leave for college.

"I can't leave you like this" she cried at my apartment.

"You may not want to, but you have to. I know this" I cried in reply.

"Promise me that you'll stay in touch. Promise me that you will answer my calls and my texts the same as you always have" she said with grief.

"I promise" I replied.

"Promise me that you'll be okay" she pleaded.

I didn't know if I would be okay, but I couldn't tell her, so I forced the tears to stop flowing from my eyes and lied. "I promise I'll be okay" I responded.

We kissed each other goodbye. When she opened the door to my apartment and slowly closed it behind her I felt as alone as I had ever been. It was because I was now truly alone.

Perhaps things would have been different between us had I said the words I love you. Perhaps things would have been different if she had said those words to me. I often wonder if it would have made a difference, but I don't know if it would have. I do know that I'll never know.

The money my dad had left me was enough to cover the rent on the apartment for a couple of months, but I didn't know what I was going to do once the money ran out. I sold what I could including the pickup truck but at most the money I now had was enough to cover the rent for three months at best.

I used the little money that I had saved from my job to pay for groceries, but I often found myself trying to sleep with my stomach grumbling. The only jobs I could find paid minimum wage and all those jobs would allow me to do was buy myself a bit more time.

I reluctantly took a job at a restaurant not too far from my apartment called "Twins." The name of the restaurant wasn't because the owners were twins but rather a not so coy synonym for tits. The outfit consisted of tight spandex shorts and a half tee shirt that barely covered my twins. It felt that at any moment my tits would burst from the shirt.

I couldn't stand the job! I felt like I was constantly being eye-fucked by every guy who I served. I was working seven days a week and struggling financially. The only good thing about the job was that I was able to eat for free.

Danielle and I stayed in touch, for a while anyway. Slowly the daily texts tricked down to a couple per week and we spoke here and there. She was a college freshman in New York City, and I was a full-time waitress in Sparks, Nevada. It wasn't like we wanted to drift apart but distance and time took its course.

I knew I needed to downsize my living accommodations, but I didn't have enough money to pay the required one month rent and one-month security while continuing to pay my rent, so I rolled the dice. I figured if I skipped a month's rent and made a partial payment here and there, I could eventually make a move.

I gambled and lost. With my feet and back aching, I slowly walked home to find an eviction notice on my door with a padlock. I begged the landlord to let me stay for even a couple of more days but all he did was allow me to go inside and grab whatever belongings I could carry. Other than my clothes and some paperwork I didn't have much else so anyway, so I packed up and went to a motel.

The motel room was tiny, damp and smelled terrible but at least it was a place to lay my head. I toyed with the notion of joining the military, but I knew I wasn't built for military life. I felt trapped and beaten down by life. I cried a lot and I mean a lot.

I didn't associate with anyone at work other than a hello at arrival and good night at departure. I was slowly saving a few dollars here and there, but the amount was never going to change my living situation. I was becoming desperate.

As if my life couldn't get any worse it did. One evening at work I was waiting on a table full of a bunch of horny and drunk middle-aged men. As I was placing their order on the table, I accidentally pushed a fork off the table.

When I bent down to pick it up a guy sitting at the end of the booth grabbed my ass.

That was it. My feet constantly hurt as did my back. I lived in a roach infested motel and I was living just above broke. I had no one to rely on. I was lonely desperate and angry. I snapped!

I slowly rose to my feet, smiled at the guy who just grabbed my ass and with all my might I slapped him so hard across the face that the entire restaurant became dead silent. I was fired on the spot!

My manager didn't give a damn that I had been sexually harassed. All he cared was that I had assaulted a loyal paying customer. I was unemployed yet again.

When I arrived at my motel room, I didn't know how I had even managed to walk there. It felt as if my mind were blank, yet my body subconsciously knew where to take me.

I spent close to a week locked in my motel room, lying in bed and crying. That was until I decided to finally drag my body out of bed, get dressed and take a walk to a liquor store. I purchased a bottle of tequila without even being asked for identification.

As soon as I walked out of the liquor store, I began to walk back to my motel room without giving a shit about what anyone thought for the first time in my life. I ripped the bottle from its paper bag, threw the bag to the floor, opened the bottle and began to drink from it in plain sight as I walked.

A few drinks from the bottle later I realized I didn't want to go back to my motel room, so I instead took a seat on the curb and continued to drink from the bottle.

I don't recall how long I sat at that curb drinking but I do know it was long enough that the sun began to set, and the bottle was more than half empty.

I was still sitting at the curb as a took another sip from the bottle when I watched a car slowly drive past me. I watched the brake lights come on, watched it make a u-turn drive past me on the other side of the street and watch it make yet another u-turn.

The car slowly drove past me and then came to a stop a few feet from where I sat. I watched the driver side door open and saw a familiar face.

"June, what are you doing?" I heard Francine ask as I shrugged my shoulders.

"Have you lost your mind? Are you trying to get arrested? Get in the car!" she commanded.

"I'm okay" I replied.

"I wasn't asking. Get in the car now!" she commanded again as she took the bottle from my hand and poured the remaining liquor out of the bottle. She helped me to my feet and put me in the passenger seat of her car.

"What are you wearing?" she asked with shock.

With slurred speech, I replied, "My old outfit. I don't need it anymore, I was fired after some drunk asshole grabbed a handful of my ass."

"I'm taking you home. Where am I going?" she asked.

"A few blocks down and then make a right" I responded.

As she drove, I could tell that was worried about me, even more so when I told her to pull into the parking lot of the motel.

"This is where you live?" she asked with concern as I slowly nodded my head.

"Thank you for the ride," I said to her as I removed myself from the car. When I closed the door, I heard the engine turn off and watched Francine get out of the car.

I walked to my room with Francine in tow and unlocked the door. When I stepped inside, Francine stepped inside behind me.

She looked around the room when suddenly a look of disgust came over her.

"What's that smell?" she asked.

"What smell?" I asked as she shook her head.

"It smells like something died in here" she replied as I laughed drunkenly and replied, "Something probably did."

"I heard about your father. I'm so sorry" she said to me as I looked at her sadly and replied, "Thanks."

Francine scanned my motel room over and again when I looked at her and said, "Thanks for the ride again. I'm sure you have somewhere to be, but it was nice seeing you again."

"Pack your clothes and get in the car" she commanded.

"Why would I do that?" I responded.

With her teeth gritted and her jaw clenched she looked at me and said with conviction, "Pack your clothes and get in the car now!"

I did as she commanded and twenty minutes later, she pulled her car into a long driveway where a beautiful home with a manicured lawn and a white picket fence stood.

"Where did you just take me?" I asked not knowing what to think as she smiled and replied, "My home."

She grabbed my packed bag from the back seat and said, "Follow me."

I followed her to the other side of a garage and up to a long staircase. She opened the door at the top of the staircase as I followed her inside.

"It's not much but you can stay here for as long as you need to," she said to me with a smile.

"Francine I can't afford to pay you to rent this place," I said sadly.

"I'm not asking you for rent. As I said, you can stay here for as long as you need" she said as she opened my bag, unpacked it and began to put my clothing away.

It was a studio apartment above her garage. It was small but cozy. There was a tiny kitchen in the corner with a stove and microwave. A small bathroom with a sink and stand up shower as well as a decent size closet.

"Are you sure?" I asked stunned as to what she was allowing me to do.

"I'm sure. Now, get some rest. I'll check in on you later" she said.

When she exited the apartment, I took a long hot shower and laid down on the futon that doubled as the living room couch.

When I heard a car pull into the driveway I rose from the futon and looked out to the driveway from a small circular window. I watched a large Mercedes come to a stop next to Francine's car as a handsome, tall man got out with two children getting out of the back seat.

I watched Francine hug and kiss her children and watched her greet her husband. I didn't know what she was saying to him, but I do know he didn't look all too happy over what was being said to him.

I couldn't remember the last time I slept so well. However, when I awoke in the morning I felt completely out of place. I exited the apartment and took a seat on the patio and gazed at my reflection present in the pool water.

"Good morning," Francine's husband said to me as he entered the backyard dressed in a suite.

"Good morning" I replied with a smile.

"I'm Francine's husband Michae," he said as I responded, "Nice to meet you, Michael."

He took a seat next to me and said, "You're welcome to stay in the apartment but there are a few rules that need to be followed. There's no drinking, drugs use of any kind and no parties without telling me or Francine first" he said firmly.

I nodded my head and replied, "I'm not much of a drinker, I don't do drugs and I wouldn't have anyone to invite to a party anyway."

"Okay then. Have a good day" he said as he arose from the seat, opened the fence door and closed it behind him. I heard him start the car and heard the car slowly back down the driveway.

I was living in Francine's garage apartment for a couple of weeks yet still had no idea as to what I was going to do with myself. It was a Monday morning as I watched television in the apartment when Francine walked in.

She looked like she was in pain and sounded like she was in pain when she said, "Good morning June."

"Are you okay?" I asked her with concern.

"Yeah, I think I just slept in the wrong position. My neck is killing me" she confessed.

"Have a seat," I said with a smile as she took a seat on the futon next to me. I rose from the futon and walked around it. I now stood behind Francine as she sat.

I slowly began to massage her shoulders and neck as she let out a gasp of relief as I massaged her.

"That feels so good. How did you learn to massage?" she asked curiously as she enjoyed the massage I was providing.

"I used to do this for my dad almost daily since I was a kid," I said with pride.

"Oh God, you have the hands of a miracle worker. You should do this for a living" she said to me.

I should do this for a living? My dad like my massage, Danielle liked my massages and now Francine was enjoying my massage. Should I do this for a living? Maybe I should do this for a living. I should do this for a living!

"Do you really think so?" I asked seeking her advice.

"Yeah, I mean you could make a decent living. I don't know about you but when I was your age making close to fifty thousand dollars a year would have been amazing" she replied.

"Can I really make that much money doing massages?" I asked curiously.

"Yeah, as long as your licensed" she replied.

"How do I get a license?" I asked.

"You would need to get certified" she replied as I finished massaging her a little over ten minutes later.

"Thank you so much, I feel better," she said with a smile as I returned her smile and asked, "Can I borrow your laptop?"

She nodded her head, left the apartment and came back a few minutes later with her laptop. She placed it on the coffee table and said, "I have a few errands to run so I'll see you in a bit."

With excitement, I used her laptop to research how to become a licensed massage therapist in Nevada and within a half hour, I felt defeated. I needed 550 hours of education and pass a test. The lowest price I could find to become licensed was a little over $8,000.

When Francine returned, she had a look of excitement on her face. "How did your research go?" she asked.

"I can't afford to become a licensed massage therapist. The most inexpensive school as a little over $8,000 and I barely have $1,000 saved. I would take a loan, but I don't have credit" I replied with sadness.

"Do you think this is something you would want to do?" she asked curiously as I nodded my head and replied, "I think so. I am good at it and I could make a decent living" I responded.

"Okay then, let's get you signed up," she said with an ear to ear smile.

"How?" I asked with confusion.

"I'm going to pay for you to go," she said with a smile.

"I can't let you do that" I responded with shock.

"Yeah, you can. You can pay me back when you get on your feet but in the meantime, you'll be my personal masseuse" she said.

I didn't want her to pay for me to become a massage therapist but what choice did I really have? It would take me forever to save up the money I needed, and I would, of course, pay her back.

"Okay, great," I said with excitement.

It was a seven-and-a-half-month program and the school offered job assistance. I could earn anywhere between $40,000 to over $60,000 a year! Not bad for a below average high school student with no college degree.

The material in the program wasn't all too difficult and I enjoyed attending the classes. For the first time in a long time, I felt that there was a light at the end of the tunnel.

I was a little over three months into the program and I enjoyed living in the garage apartment at Francine's. As promised, I gave Francine massages whenever she wanted them.

It was a Thursday afternoon and Francine was beyond stressed out. She and Michael decided that they would again open an ice cream shop but this time around they would purchase a building so a landlord could never again take her out of business.

They had just purchased a building and it was being renovated. I could tell from her body language that she needed a massage in the worst way.

"Massage?" I asked her with a smile, and she nodded her head and replied, "In the worst way."

We went into the garage apartment and she entered the tiny bathroom to undress as I removed the used massage table that I purchased online for a steal.

I set the mood as she exited the bathroom wrapped in a large white towel. She laid face down on the table as I massage every inch of her back, neck, arms, and legs. As I always did when I was finished with her back, I told her to roll over so I could massage her arms, legs, and temples.

As I massaged her arms, I leaned my body over her. My tits were above her face as I continued to massage her arms. She was biting down on her bottom lip as I continued the massage.

Out of nowhere she grabbed the back of my head and pulled my face toward hers. We began to French kiss when she suddenly stopped kissing me and removed herself from the massage table.

"I'm sorry, I didn't mean to do that. I don't know what came over me" she said with embarrassment.

"It's okay. It was nice" I replied with a smile. I wasn't being dishonest. It was nice to kiss her. It had been so long, so I had been kissed and kissed another person back.

She had a pained look on her face as she looked at me.

"What's the matter?" I asked as she looked at me with the same look, she once did in her office in the back of the ice cream shop.

She unwrapped her towel and I watched it fall to the floor. I would be lying if I said that I didn't have a sexual attraction to Francine any longer. The truth of the matter was that it never went away.

There she stood completely nude. Her long flowing black hair, her beautiful blue eyes, her amazing huge tits, and her bare pussy.

Without hesitating for a second, I quickly walked to her as we again began to French kiss. As we kissed, I began to play with her nipples which became rock hard. I could tell she was becoming more and more excited by the way she was kissing me.

She pulled me into her by placing her hands on my ass. She gently moved her hands up and down on my ass as we continued to kiss.

I slowly moved my right hand to in between her legs as we kissed and touched her. She was so wet!

I walked her toward the foot of the massage table and laid her down. I kissed and licked her breasts and began to suck on her nipple as I played with her wet pussy.

Like a girl possessed I quickly placed my head in between her legs and tasted her pussy for the first time. She had a different taste then Danielle, but I enjoyed the taste none the less.

"June…" she exhaled in pleasure as I licked her clit and spread the lips of her pussy apart. I kissed and sucked on her pussy lips and in between as I played with her clit.

"Don't stop" she pleaded although I had no intention of stopping. As she began to pant her entire body began to squirm as I ate her pussy with more and more passion.

I stopped eating her and began to furiously rub her clit with my right hand as I rubbed her tits and nipples with my left hand.

She was panting until she started taking quick short inhales of oxygen and small quick exhales over and again. Her body began to convulse as she cried out in pleasure. As she orgasmed, I continued to furiously rub her clit. I slowly stopped rubbing her clit and laid myself on top of her as we kissed passionately for a long while.

"We shouldn't do that again. I'm so sorry I didn't stop you" she said to me with a pained look present on her face.

"I wanted to do that to you since the time you did it to me," I said with a smirk.

"Okay, but we can't get sexually involved. It's wrong" she said as I removed myself from her and she slid off the massage table.

"I know" I replied.

I know Francine and I agreed that becoming sexually involved was wrong and we did our best to make sure that nothing more happened between us. We fought ourselves for a little over a month until we could no longer bear it.

I began to give her sexually seductive massages a couple of times per week which turned into almost every other day which led to no more massages but rather sexual encounters almost every other day.

Our sexual conduct became worse when the renovations to the ice cream shop were completed. Although I was now a licensed massage therapist, I found myself again working with Francine at an ice cream shop more often than I was at the massage spa I was working at.

Almost every night before we left the shop before closing, we wound up naked and fucking each other on her desk, on the counter and even inside the freezer. We couldn't keep our hands off each other. Ice cream, whip cream, and even candy were consumed off each other's bodies.

Our relationship was strictly sexual. We both knew what our relationship was. She was a wife and mother and I was a teenager. We had close to a twenty-year age gap between us. Our relationship could never ever go beyond what it was, but I was fine with it. Having these trysts with Francine made the longing for Danielle to slowly but surely subside.

I had been living in the garage apartment at Francine's for a well over a year and had been having sexual rendezvous after rendezvous with her for months when it all suddenly came to an end.

It was late on a Friday night when I heard Michael screaming at Francine in the driveway just outside the garage. My curiosity got the best of me so I made my way down the long staircase and to the side of the garage so I could hear what was being said.

"I'm not blind Francine. I know what's going on and it's going to stop!" he seethed.

"You always knew I had this side to me. It didn't stop you from marrying me and having kids with me!" she snapped back.

"You're right I did know, and I thought we had an understanding. I always said I would turn a blind eye as long as it wasn't thrown in my face but you're not keeping your part of the agreement" he said lowering his voice.

"Most guys would kill for this. Not once, not once have you ever offered to join in with me and another woman" she said also lowering her voice.

"I love you and I don't want to share you with anyone. Yeah, most guys would kill for this but I'm not most guys. Besides, June is not a woman, she a kid for God's sake, Francine" he said with conviction.

"She's not a kid, Michael," she said with conviction in reply.

"Francine, she can't even legally buy or drink alcohol. You are a thirty-eight-year-old wife and mother. I don't want to say or do this but it's me or her. She either goes or I do. I can't live like this" he said to her as serious as a heart attack.

"Michael?" she pleaded as he said forcefully, "When I agreed to let her stay here, I didn't think it would be for so long. It's close to two years. As I said, me or her Francine, me or her."

After everything she had done for me, I never meant to interfere in her marriage. Regardless of what we were doing sexually, I knew how much she truly loved him. I knew what I had to do. I couldn't let her have to tell me to leave, I needed to do it on my own as if it were my decision.

As they continued to talk, I went back into the apartment and began to pack my clothes. As I was finishing packing my things Francine walked into the apartment. I could tell that she was beyond upset.

"What are you doing?" she asked me with surprise.

"Thank you for everything you've done for me. I don't know what my life would be like if it weren't for your kindness and generosity but it's time for me to go. I promise I'll pay you the rest of the money I owe you as soon as possible" I told her.

"Where are you going?" she asked with concern.

"I'm going to get a hotel room for a couple of days until I find an apartment of my own. This place has been great and all but it's a bit cramped" I said to her with a smile.

I know she knew I had overheard her conversation with Michael. With tears in her eyes, she asked, "Will you be okay?" as I nodded my head and replied, "More than okay, Fran."

She helped me load the little Honda I had purchased a week earlier and suddenly went into the house leaving me in the driveway by myself.

Francine returned a few minutes later with an envelope in hand. She handed me the envelope as I slowly opened it.

The envelope was full of cash! "Fran, what is this?" I asked.

"The massage school was my gift to you. Inside is the $3,800 you paid me" she said with a teary-eyed smile.

As I attempted to reply she pressed her index finger to my lips. She kissed me on my cheek and hugged me tightly.

"Goodbye June," she said full of emotion. She didn't say "See you later," "Stay in touch," or "Talk you soon." She said the word, "Goodbye." I knew this would be the last time I ever saw her. I would be lying if I said I wasn't upset but I more than understood.

"Goodbye, Francine," I said with tears forming in my eyes as I entered my car, turned the engine over and backed down the driveway for the final time.

All these years later when I think about Francine, I can't help but smile. I often wonder what her life is like these days, but some things are better left to the unknown.

With the money, Francine had given back to me in combination with the money I had saved while working at the small massage spa I had more than enough to find a small studio apartment. I didn't want to sign a lease, so the landlord charges me an extra $200 a month for a month to month rental agreement.

My boss, Harold, was a nice guy and treated us massage therapists well but I couldn't help but notice that business wasn't quite what it was when I first started working there. A little over a month later I wasn't the least bit surprised when he told us that he was closing the store.

It took me a couple of weeks, but I was able to gain employment at a luxurious spa resort. It was close to a golf club and although the split with the spa was more than I was accustomed to, the number of clients was much greater which meant I was making more money.

I had been employed there for a little over a month when something happened, I couldn't have ever imagined! I had finished massaging the backside of an older man when I told him to roll over. When he rolled over, I massage his temples and arms and then walked to the foot of the massage table so I could massage his legs.

As I massaged his legs and worked my way up his legs, I could see his dick becoming hard underneath the towel. I didn't think much of it as this was a common occurrence but what happened next was far from the usual.

As I continued to massage his upper inside thigh, he removed the towel exposing his rock-hard cock.

"Okay, I'm finished. Have a great day" I said to him.

"You're finished?" he asked me with confusion as I nodded my head and said again, "I'm finished."

"You're not going to finish me off?" he asked with even more confusion.

I quickly shook my head with disgust as he became angry. "Harold told me to ask for you, Junie and I did. I have the $200 tip so get to work darling."

"My name is June, not Junie! As I said, I'm finished!" I snapped and quickly exited the room.

I felt sick and angry at the same time. I knew Junie but not well, but I decided that I was going to confront her. I was a massage therapist, not a happy ending specialist!

I went outside to get some fresh air when my boss asked me to come inside. followed him into the office and was told to sit down.

"June, I need to understand why Mr. Samuels was so upset when he left. He's a been a loyal customer and I would like to assure that he continues to be so."

"Steven, he expected me to jerk him off for $200" I confessed.

"I don't see the issue June," told me without batting an eye.

"What?!" I seethed.

"We are in the customer service business meaning your job is to service the client" he vented.

"What are you saying to me right now?!" I again seethed.

"What I'm saying is that it's your job to give the customer what he wants" he responded as a matter of fact.

"So, you're good with your massage therapist jerking off clients?" I asked with a sick feeling.

"June you're a young girl so let me educate you. These men don't come here just for massages. They come here for release. Release from their wives, businesses, kids, and stress. Jerking a client off is just part of the business. You're either in or you're out. The choice is yours" he said coldly.

I didn't want to lose my job. I was making a good living, so I looked him square in the eye and replied, "Okay, I'm in."

I left his office and quickly made my way to the back exit. I took a quick breath so I could regain my composure. I stood there for a moment as I watched Junie park her small BMW convertible.

"Hey June," she said as she walked past me.

"Junie, can I please talk to you for a minute?" I asked.

"Yeah, what's up?" she asked,

"I just finished a session with a guy, and he expected me to jerk him off for $200," I said with disgust.

She let out a small laugh and replied, "And?"

"And what?" I asked with a stunned tone.

She again laughed and replied, "It's just business June."

"You jerk off clients?" I asked her with surprise.

"And more," she said with a wink and a smile.

From my body language, she could tell that I was stunned. She let out a small laugh and looked at me as she shook her head.

"June, it's just business. $200 for a hand job, $400 for a covered blow job, $$700 for an uncovered blow job and full service for $1,000" she said to me with a mischievous smile.

I couldn't believe what she had just told me! I felt my face become flush and I felt my knees weaken.

"You are so innocent" she laughed.

"Listen, if you want to make real money you need to come to terms with what it is you and I do for a living. I made over $4,000 last week, not including our shitty split" she said to me with pride.

"Full service?" I asked as I almost became ill at the thought.

"It's not bad at all. The secret is to get them so worked up before you fuck that they cum quick. If you do what you're supposed to do it will last for well under a minute. I've had guys come in less than thirty seconds. Just make sure they don't fuck you without a condom" she said again with pride.

"$4,000 last week?" I asked in shock.

"Yeah, not including my private clients. $2,000 a pop. If I include them, I made close to $10,000 last week alone" she responded.

"I'm going to be sick" I confessed.

"June you're hot. I hate to admit it, but you are way hotter than I am. I'm sure you could pull in $10,000 in a shit week" she said with a smile.

I looked at her and said, "Tell Steven I quit" as I quickly got into my car and drove home.

What had I done? Did I enter some sort of backdoor to venture down the road of prostitution?! I knew that things happened in the industry but never imagined that I would ever come across it. Had I known that this was a major part of the profession I would have never decided to take the career path.

A couple of days later I decided that my best course of action was to go into business for myself. I would offer on-site massages for a reasonable fee. Without having to take a split I could charge less per client and make more money. I excitedly posted on a bunch of online classified sites using the name Paige Anderson.

The business was nonexistent. I did get email and phone inquiries, but it was all from guys who wanted full- service sessions. I sat in my apartment when I realized the reason that Harold went out of business was that we didn't offer anything above and beyond a massage.

Clients expected to be presented with an offer above and beyond a massage. When they weren't, they didn't come back. If you have no repeat customers, you have no business.

I know I was a lesbian. I could find a guy to be attractive, but I would never do anything sexual with a guy. I wouldn't jerk a guy off let alone let a guy fuck me. The thought of watching the cum shoot out of a cock in front of me made me cringe.

However, as a lesbian, I wouldn't have an issue giving a massage to a woman and getting her off. I initially laughed at the thought as I didn't think there was a market for such a service until I did some online research.

Happy ending massages for women was becoming an actual thing! The more research I did the more that I became intrigued with the idea. The service normally consisted of men getting a woman off but what if there was a market for a woman who wanted to be massaged and brought to orgasm by another woman?!

I enjoyed giving those types of massages to both Danielle and Francine so why wouldn't I enjoy giving them to women for a fee? I had nothing to lose and everything to gain so I decided to travel down the road of the unknown.

I went back onto those same classified websites I had previously posted on and placed ads for onsite "Yoni Massage by Paige" for an hour session for $300.

I didn't know what to expect and was stunned when I receive an email inquiry for a woman named Veronica that didn't live all too far from my apartment that included a phone number.

I dialed the number and the phone rang a few times when a nervous sounding female voice answered, "Hello."

"Hi, this is Paige Anderson. I understand that you would like a yoni session this evening" I responded.

"Yes," the voice replied sounding even more nervous than before.

"Veronica, when would you like the massage?" I inquired as she replied, "Now if you're available."

I replied that I was and was given the address to her location. I put my massage table in my car and entered the address into my GPS. A few minutes later I arrived at a small house.

I exited my car and went to the front door. I waited for a few seconds when an attractive woman nervously opened the door.

"Hi, Veronica?" I asked as she nervously smiled and nodded her head.

"I'm Paige. It's very nice to meet you" I said with a smile as she replied, "Likewise. I just need to get my massage table from my car and set up. It will only take a few minutes."

She smiled nervously at me as she went inside the house leaving the front door open. I went to my car, placed my bag over my shoulder and carried the massage table inside the house. Veronica told me to set up in the living room and it only took me a few minutes to set up.

"There's no need to be nervous," I said with a reassuring and calming voice.

"I can't help it. I've never done anything like this before" she said to me in reply.

"There's a first time for everything" I replied with a smirk.

"So, should I undress and put on a towel?" she asked.

I'm not going to lie. I wanted to see her naked. She was a bigger woman. She wasn't fat but thick if that makes sense.

"No towel is fine" I replied with a smile. I watched her undress and when she removed her bra, I felt myself become excited. She had huge tits and I mean huge! Her nipples were large and pink. In the nude, she walked over to a small end table and handed me three $100 bills.

She nervously climbed onto the table face down as I began my normal massage. I could feel the knots in her shoulders as I massaged her.

"You have a ton of knots. What do you do for a living?" I asked as she replied, "Pharmaceutical sales."

I massage her neck, back, arms and legs but left her ass for last. I applied more massage oil to my hands and slowly began to massage her ass muscles. From her body language, I knew she liked how I was massaging her.

"Roll-over" I commanded as she rolled her body over and now laid on her back.

I massage her temples, her arms, and legs. I was beyond sexually aroused as I made my way to the head of the massage table. I applied a bit more massage oil to my hands and began to gently massage her tits.

As I massage her tits, I knew she was becoming sexually aroused from her breathing and the way she was moving her body. I massaged down her stomach and stopped. I made my way to the side of the massage table and gently pulled her legs apart exposing her pussy.

When I touched her pussy, she jerked her body slightly and let out a gasp. "Relax Veronica," I said to her as she opened her eyes and smiled at me.

Using the tips of my fingers, I massaged her pussy in a circular motion as I alternated the amount of pressure I was using. I pushed and pulled on her clit and then tugged and rolled it. I gently tapped her pussy and then alternated between fast and slow.

I hooked my finger and gently inserted my finger into her as I tickled her clit and moved my finger in and out of her. I stopped playing with her clit as I fingered her and gently rubbed her nipples. When I knew she was close to cumming I slowed down and then picked up the pace until I knew she was again close to cumming when I again slowed down.

The experience was exhilarating. It felt as if I was controlling her entire body with each slight movement of my hands and fingers. When I brought her close to climax for and down again for the fourth time, I decided it was not time to make her cum.

I began to finger fuck her with quick short movements with my right hand as I furiously rubbed her clit with my left hand until she screamed out with pleasure.

She could barely catch her breath as she opened her eyes and looked at me with embarrassment.

I smiled and said, "All done" as she slowly closed and opened her eyes.

"I wasn't sure what to expect but that was fantastic," she said in between breaths.

"I'm glad you liked it" I replied as she removed herself from the table, went into her purse and handed me another $100 dollars.

"Thank you, Veronica," I said with a smile as she returned my smile and asked, "Can you come over the same time and day next week?"

I nodded my head and replied, "It would be my pleasure."

When I arrived at my apartment, I felt euphoria. I counted the $400 over and again and couldn't believe what I had just done to earn the money.

All I did was provide a normal massage and play with a woman's pussy until she came for $400!

The feeling of euphoria slowly dissipated as four months later my business seemed to be stagnant. I had a handful of steady clients and a bunch of one-timers. I was barely making $5,000 a month but I wanted more. The feeling of counting cold hard cash in my hands was intoxicating and I wanted more.

Where could I go where I could make more money? I wanted to make Junie money but with women! Viva Las Vegas! I exclaimed to myself.

Two short weeks later I made the drive from Sparks, Nevada to my new apartment in Las Vegas, Nevada. I created a website, had business cards created and had visions of grandeur.

At the time I thought to move to Las Vegas was the best things I could have possibly done. The business was booming and I was making more money than I ever imagined I could. A bad month was close to $10,000 and a great month was close to $20,000. I paid income taxes on my standard fee of $300 but the tips were all in cash and all mine.

I decided to step my game up and make myself more attractive. I joined a gym, hired a personal trainer and began to sculpt my body. I ate healthily, exercised, made sure was hair was always done and had my nails manicured weekly.

I had been in business in Las Vegas for a little over six months when I went down a road, I never thought I would travel down.

I remember this as if it happened an hour ago. I had an appointment for a woman named Mandy at the Venetian. When I entered her room, her demeanor was not what I had become accustomed to. She was calm, cool, collected and stunning.

She was short but had long flowing brown hair and the lightest brown eyes I had ever seen. She was dressed in a fluffy pink robe and wasn't nervous at all as she handed me my $300-dollar fee.

She had a huge diamond ring on her ring finger that she removed and placed on the nightstand. She removed her robe and smiled at me. She was by far one of the hottest if not the hottest woman I had ever laid eyes on!

"Your turn," she said which threw me off my game.

"Say again?" I asked with confusion as she smiled at me and repeated the words, "Your turn."

"I'm sorry but there seems to be a misunderstanding. I don't remove my clothing" I said to her.

She let out a giggle as she looked at me. She walked over to the nightstand, opened the drawer, took hold of something and handed it to me.

I counted the money to discover she had just handed me an additional $200.

She smiled and again said, "Your turn."

I stood silently for a moment as I tried to process what just happened. She just gave me an additional $200 to give her a nude massage. What's the harm? I thought to myself as I removed my clothing and now stood before her nude.

"Very nice," she said as she licked her lips and ran her hand over my stomach.

"Forget the table. Massage me on the bed" she said.

I could tell she enjoyed every moment of the massage I was giving her. However, this massage would be unlike any other I had ever given.

When she rolled over, I couldn't stand at the head of the bed as it was against the wall. I instead placed my body over hers. I was kneeling above her head as I continued the massage with my pussy hovering over her face.

As I massage down her stomach, I felt her hand contact my pussy. Before I knew what was happening, she was rubbing my pussy in a circular motion. It felt great and I didn't want her to stop.

I began to massage her pussy and as I did what happened next was not what I was expecting. She wrapped her arms around my waist and pushed my crotch toward her mouth. Before I could process what was happening, she was eating my pussy.

I moaned in pleasure as she ate me and without hesitation, I placed my face over her pussy and began to eat her pussy. I was now in a 69 position and eating her pussy as she ate my pussy. During the act now once did I feel what was happening shouldn't be. It felt natural and felt right.

As she penetrated my pussy with her finger and began to finger fuck me it felt so good that I exclaimed, "Just like that...don't stop...make me cum."

Did she ever! A stranger, a woman I didn't know existed until a little over an hour ago, a woman who hired me for a yoni massage had just given me the most intense orgasm of my life. When I finally made her cum, I was exhausted and drenched in sweat.

"Thank you," she said with relief as she got out of the bed, went back into the drawer on the nightstand and handed me an additional $500 and asked for my business card. I handed her my card without hesitation.

"You can take a shower if you want but please be quick. I need to shower myself and get ready to walk down the aisle" she said to me. I was stunned!

"Thanks, but I think I'm going to head out now" I replied as I got dressed, grab my bag and massage table and left the room and hotel. On the drive back to my apartment I could feel my pussy still throbbing from the orgasm I had.

When I arrived at my apartment, I counted the money over and again. $1,000 dollars, $1,000 dollars! I had sex with a smoking hot woman, and she paid me $1,000 to do so.

I had a moment of clarity. The thought of Junie letting men fuck her for $1,000 had disgusted me but it shouldn't have! She was straight and letting a guy fuck her was the same as me, a lesbian, fucking a woman. Not just any woman, one of the hottest girls I had ever laid eyes on. I had an amazing orgasm and got paid a cool $1,000 in cash.

I didn't know it at the time but the simple act of handing my business card to Mandy opened the floodgates to my business. I was making a ton of money and loved every waking second of my existence!

One year to the day that I had the Mandy encounter I was driving an Audi, had a boatload of money in the bank, over $25,000 in cash in a box under my bed and had a wardrobe filled with designer clothes, shoes, and bags in my new high-rise apartment.

My life was unlike anything I could have ever imagined yet when I was alone and laid my head down for the night, Danielle was all I could think of.

Why? I hadn't spoken to her in years, but my mind constantly wondered. Was she still at Columbia? Was she happy? Did she ever think of me? How did we lose contact? What was she doing? Did she wonder the same about me? I had thought I was over her, but I was lying to myself the entire time.

It was just past 12:30 AM on a Sunday and I remember being upset that I didn't have a session for Saturday night. I looked at myself in the mirror and spoke to my own reflection. I've never looked better! I can't look any better than I do now. Why don't I have a session? I vented.

As if it were destiny my cell phone rang with a number that displayed unavailable.

I answered the phone, "This is Paige. How may I help you?"

The person who responded was a woman with a thick and heavy Russian accent.

"Hello, Paige. My name is Svetlana Orlov. I would like to know what your fee is for an in-call" she responded.

"My apologies, but I don't do in-calls" I replied.

"I have $20,000 that says you do" she immediately replied.

I thought for a moment and then shook my head. "You must be mistaken. There is no amount of money that you can offer that would allow an in-call" I explained.

"Okay, $50,000 then" she replied.

$50,000?! It didn't feel right. Why would some random woman offer me $50,000 for an in -call? It was an absurd amount of money, but I couldn't risk allowing anyone and I mean anyone to know where I lived.

"You must be mistaken. There is no amount of money that you can offer that would allow an in-call" I explained again.

"Very well. You come to me in one hour. Nobu Villa, Caesar's Palace. Do not be late" she replied.

"Nobu Villa? Did you say Nobu Villa?" I asked with disbelief.

"As I said, Nobu Villa, Caesar's Palace. Don't be late. One hour" she replied.

"I won't be late but who referred you to me?" I responded.

"I will tell you when you get here. As I said, one hour, Nobu Villa at Caesar's Palace" as she ended the call.

I rummaged through my closet trying to find an outfit worthy of Nobu Villa. Who was she? Who gave her my number? It all seemed so strange to me.

I find an outfit that I felt would be appropriate and drove to Caesar's Palace. My car was parked by the valet and I made my way to the concierge desk.

"Good morning, I'm here to see Svetlana Orlov," I said to the man with a smile.

"Your name, please" he replied.

"Paige Anderson" I answered.

"One moment please" he replied. He picked up the phone and spoke into the receiver, "Ms. Orlov. I have a Ms. Paige Anderson before me" He nodded his head and smiled at me.

"Ms. Orlov is expecting you. Please follow me" he said.

When I arrived at the door to the room a tall man greeted me. He too had a heavy Russian accent.

"Please, follow me," he said. As I followed the man I was in awe of the room. It was the very epitome of luxury. I continued to follow the man to an outside terrace the overlooked the Vegas strip.

"Ms. Orlov will be with you momentarily," he said to me as he showed me to an outdoor couch. He exited the patio leaving me alone on the terrace.

A few minutes later a beautiful, slender older woman walked out to the terrace. She seemed to be in her late forties and was dressed exquisitely with a large diamond necklace around her neck and diamond earrings hanging from her ears.

"Ms. Wynter, it is a pleasure to meet you. I am Svetlana" she said as she took a seat across from me.

"What did you just call me?" I asked with a combination of fear and suspicion.

"Ms. Wynter as in Ms. June Wynter. It is your name is it not?" she replied.

"How do you know my name?" I asked nervously.

"No need to worry my dear. Where are my manners?" she asked herself as she handed me three $100 bills.

"How do you know my name?" I asked her again with ever building fear.

She let out a laugh and responded, "As I said, relax my dear. I just want to talk. I would like to get to know you a bit better."

I guess she could tell I was scared as she looked at me and smiled.

"It is my job to know who you are. You have built quite the little business in a quite short time and I'm intrigued" she said to me.

I swallowed hard and asked, "Who referred you to me?"

She shook her head and replied, "No one."

"I'm going to go," I said but the look she gave me stopped me dead in my tracks as I again found myself sitting down on the outdoor couch.

"You may leave if you wish but it's in both of our interests if you stay. I've been looking for someone like you for a very long time" she said with a smile.

"Someone like me?" I asked in reply.

"Ms. Wynter are you familiar with the magical creature knowns as the unicorn?" she asked as I nodded my head.

She again smiled and replied, "You may be my unicorn, my dear."

For whatever reason when she said I may be her unicorn it put me at ease. No, it wasn't because she referred to me as a mythical horse with a horn it was because a unicorn is highly desirable and hard to obtain if not impossible to obtain.

"Why do you call me here?" I asked with curiosity.

"Consider this an interview. Should you have accepted the money I offered for the in-call you would not be here right now" she said with a smirk.

"It was a test?" I replied as she smiled and replied, "A test you passed."

She rose from her seat and sat next to me on the outdoor couch.

"You are very smart my dear, smarter than most in this business of ours. You formed a company and from that company, you filed two doing business as certificates. One for Yoni Massage by Paige and the other Paige Anderson. You drive a fancy car but not so fancy as to draw attention to yourself. You rent a luxurious apartment but an apartment that would be in reach of those who earn a good living which you are easily surpassing. Please tell me, when you receive an inquiry from a new client what do you do?"

I smiled and responded, "I use Google to check the phone number that I've been called from. If I can't trace it to the address I don't go to the appointment. I use Google Earth to check the address I was given to make sure it's safe. I always ask if someone referred them to me. If they say yes I ask questions about the person who they say referred me."

She clapped her hands together and smiled. "Beautiful and smart, a natural unlike I have seen before."

"Why am I your unicorn?" I asked with intrigue.

"You are young, beautiful and smart. You have built quite a business for yourself in a short period of time and you cater to women only" she said with conviction.

"With that, I may be your unicorn?" I asked as I raised my eyebrows.

"Perhaps but a few more questions please. I called you from an unavailable number yet here you sit. Why?" she asked.

I smiled and replied, "We didn't speak of anything incriminating during our conversation. I never told you what my fee was. I'm sure that if you were law enforcement or wanted to murder me you wouldn't be here in the Nobu Villa."

"Who is your best client?" she asked with anticipation.

I smiled and replied, "I can't tell you that. Discretion is guaranteed."

She again clapped her hands together, smiled and said, "Please, follow me."

I followed her from the outdoor terrace into a large bathroom that had a chandelier, two sinks, a lounge chair, and a large circular tub.

"Please Ms. Wynter, remove your clothes. I need to see you," she said to me stone-faced.

Without a thought, I removed my shoes, took off my dress, panties, and bra. now stood before her in the nude.

"Raise your arms" she commanded as I complied. She slowly walked around me and then said, "Arms down." I again did as she commanded.

She ran her hand up and down my stomach and slowly lifted each of my tits. She walked around me, ran her hands up and down my ass cheeks and squeezed them.

She smiled at me and said, "Perfect tits, flat and muscular stomach and a firm yet voluptuous ass" as she now stood directly in front of me.

"Thank you," I said to Svetlana as she smiled and nodded her head.

"Put this on" she commanded as she handed me a robe and I again did as she said.

I followed her out of the bathroom and into the living room of the hotel room that had a large flat screen television on the wall, a beige sectional and an amazing marble table.

"Sit there" she commanded as I again did what she said.

Svetlana grabbed a cell phone off the coffee table, said something in Russian and then ended the call. A couple of minutes later the man who had greeted me at the door entered the living room with an amazingly hot girl.

She was tall, slender, had huge tits, long blonde hair, and amazing light blue eyes. Her face was angelic. She was wearing a pair of jeans, sneaker, and a tight tee shirt. I was immediately attracted to her.

Svetlana again said something in Russian as the man exited the living room leaving me, the girl and Svetlana in the room.

"Ms. Whyte, Ms. Wilson. Ms. Wilson, Ms. Whyte" she said as the girl looked at me and shook her head.

"Now ladies, please follow me," Svetlana said as we both followed her into a large luxurious bedroom with a king size bed, dresser, couch, and chair.

Svetlana smiled at me and said, "Another part of the interview. You will do to Ms. Wilson as you do to your clients."

I felt like laughing as I thought to myself "I would do this for free!" but I used every ounce of strength in my body to prevent myself from doing so.

"See you shortly," Svetlana said as she exited the bedroom and closed the door behind her.

The girl looked at me, rolled her eyes and locked onto my face. "The only reason I agreed to this is that Svet is paying me my normal fee and then some. I'm as straight as they come and the thought of you touching me is making my skin crawl, but business is business so do what you do" she said to me with disgust.

"I'm Paige," I said as she laughed and said, "You mean June."

"You are?" I asked.

"I'm Sylvia to your Paige and Jane to your June. I'm also the thoroughbred of this stable. I'm numero uno, the top of the pyramid, the cream of the crop, the best of the very best." she replied sarcastically.

"Good to know" I replied with a smile.

"Do you feel it necessary to look at me that way?" she asked as she shook her head.

"What way?" I asked as she immediately replied, "Like you want to fuck the brains out my head."

"Sorry" I replied in a low voice.

She let out a sarcastic laugh as she began to undress. I felt like a kid waiting to open a Christmas present! I watched her remove her sneakers, socks, jeans, shirt, bra, and panties. What stood before me was as close to perfection as I had ever seen.

Her tits were huge yet perky. Her stomach was flat and muscular. There didn't seem to be an ounce of fat on her body! Best of all her pussy was completely bare.

Of course, I didn't want her to be nude all by herself, so I untied my robe, removed it and placed it on the dresser.

When she looked at my nude body, she nodded her head in a way that told me she approved which was solidified when she said, "Nice."

As we both gazed at each other's nude bodies Svetlana suddenly entered the bedroom with my massage bag. She placed the bag at the foot of the bed and took a seat in the chair.

"Now that you too are a bit more familiar, Ms. Whyte, proceed," she said.

"You're going to watch?" I asked as she replied, "Yes" in Russian.

"Okay. Jane lay down on the bed face down, please" I said as Jane laid her body onto the king size bed.

I removed a massage oil from my bag and placed it on the bed. I then placed the bag on the dresser.

As soon as climbed onto the bed and kneeled over Jane's body she tensed up and when I say tensed up, I mean tensed up!

I leaned over her, making sure my tits touched her back as I whispered into her ear, "Relax. I promise I'm going to make you feel great."

Jane took in a deep breath and exhaled. "Whatever," she said with a sarcastic voice.

As I began to massage her shoulders, I could feel the tension. Not only in her shoulders but in her entire body.

"You're so tense. I need you to relax. Can you try and relax for me?" I asked as she again took in a deep breath, exhaled and replied, "Whatever."

As I massaged her body, I could feel the tension melting away with every move of my hands. I poured a little oil over her back and continued to massage every square inch of her close to a perfect body. With each feeling of her body, I could feel myself becoming more turned on.

I massaged her ass, down both her legs and massaged her feet. "Jane, roll over onto your back," I said to her with a calming voice, as I now stood on the side of the bed.

I poured a little massage oil on her tits and stomach and began to massage her. As I touched her breast's she let out a moan of pleasure. I massaged down her stomach and made my way to the foot of the bed.

I began massaging her calf muscles and gently spread her legs as I climbed onto the bed and kneeled in between her legs. As I gazed at her beautiful pink pussy, I wanted nothing more than to taste her.

I applied a small amount of massage oil to my hands and rubbed them together. It was now showtime!

I massaged her pussy in a circular motion using the tips of my fingers, alternating the amount of pressure. I pushed and pulled on her clit and then tugged and rolled it. I gently tapped her pussy and then alternated between fast and slow over and again.

Her breathing was becoming erratic and I knew I was performing well. As I massaged her pussy, I watched Jane lick her lips as she began to rub her own tits.

I placed myself over her face in a kneeling position, leaned my body forward and placed my face inches away from her pussy. I blew gently on her pussy which made her body shiver.

I hooked my finger and gently inserted it into her as I tickled her clit with the fingers on my other hand. As I moved my finger in and out of her she let out a cry of passion. I finger fucked fast then slow, fast then slow over and again bringing her to the edge of orgasm only to pull back each time.

"Mmm…uh…fuck…shit…eat my pussy! Eat me!" she cried out. She didn't have to ask again as I removed my finger from her pussy and buried my face in it. As I licked her clit and moved my tongue across the lips of her pussy, she swayed her hips aggressively into my face.

As I ate her pussy, she wrapped her arms around my waist and pulled my pussy down to her face. Was she about to do what I thought she was about to do? Oh yeah! When I felt her tongue touch my pussy, I almost completely lost it!

Here I was in the 69 position with a hot girl who was supposedly straight as an arrow furiously licking my pussy. I rolled us over so that I was now beneath her. She stopped licking my pussy and began to ride my face as she braced herself on my legs.

She was frantically grinding her hips and pussy across my face and tongue. She began to move faster and faster until she came as loud as any girl I had ever gotten off. I continued to eat her pussy as she orgasmed and only stopped because she removed herself from my face.

My face was drenched in her juices as I opened my eyes to find Jane now sitting on the side of the bed staring at a smiling Svetlana. When Jane looked at me, she wasn't smiling at all. She had a super serious look and gazed at as if angry. I didn't know if she was angry at me or at her self when she abruptly got off the bed, grabbed her clothes and quickly left the bedroom.

"Ms. Whyte, please feel free to shower and dress. When you're finished meet me outside on the terrace" she said as she too exited the room.

I grabbed my clothes, went into the bathroom, took a quick shower, got dressed, exited the bathroom and met Svetlana outside on the terrace. She was sitting on the outdoor couch with a bottle of champagne and two glasses.

I sat next to her as she poured two glasses of champagne and handed me one. We clinked glasses and each took a sip of the champagne.

"How did I do?" I asked knowing full well I had performed exceptionally well.

Svetlana smiled at me and began, "I've been in this business for a very long time and have been seeking one like you for a long time. I want you to work for me" she said with seriousness.

"Thank you but I'm doing pretty well on my own" I replied.

"Why did you have the encounter with Jane then Ms. Whyte?" she asked curiously.

"I wanted to do that," I said with a laugh which brought a smile and then a laugh from Svetlana.

"Ms. Whyte, I know you are doing well on your own but what I offer will not only make you wealthy but will allow you to work less. It's wise to work smarter than harder, wouldn't you agree?" she asked.

I took a sip of the champagne and replied, "Usually is but as I said, I'm doing quite well on my own."

"I will pay you a fee of $20,000 for each liaison. You will travel the world, enjoy the finest cuisine world has to offer and you will work at most a handful of times per month. You will have all the free time you would like to enjoy the fruit of your labor" she said with a smile as she took a sip of her champagne.

"$20,000?" I asked with disbelief.

"I guarantee my clients confidentiality. Is this an issue for you Ms. Whyte?" she asked as I slowly shook my head.

"You may discuss our clients with no one, other than myself and your colleagues. Is this an issue?" she asked as I again slowly shook my head.

"Our clientele consists of mostly those who are in the public light. Those who enjoy the company of a woman from time to time and those who are intrigued by the thought of being touched by a woman. Confidentiality is of the utmost importance and there are serious repercussions for those who are unable to abide by my rules" she said stone-faced.

"What are you saying?" I asked.

"Ms. Whyte, who would come looking for you should you be unable to abide by my rules?" she asked with conviction.

"I don't have anyone" I replied with a tinge of fear.

"Do we have an understanding, Ms. Whyte?" she asked as I nodded my head in agreement.

"Very well," she said as she handed me a cell phone.

"When this rings you answer it and travel when and where I tell you," she said stone-faced.

"Okay," I nervously replied.

She smiled and sipped her champagne. "You will be paid via a check from one of my companies. To the outside world, you will be a very successful corporate recruiter when in reality...well, you know" she said with a smirk.

"Where is the company located?" I asked.

"Los Angeles" she replied.

"How did you find out about me?" I asked with intrigue.

"That is not important Ms. Whyte. What is important is that I did find you. Will you accept my job offering?" she asked.

"Can I stay in Las Vegas?" I asked.

"If you wish. You may leave anywhere in the country you choose. However, I am to know when and where should you choose to relocate" she replied.

"Can I think about this?" I asked.

She smiled and replied, "You have thirty seconds, Ms. Whyte. Tick tock."

Even with paying taxes on the fee amount there would still be cash tips. I could go out three times a month and make double what I was bringing in on my best months. I didn't have anyone in my life let alone anyone that I would tell about my meetings even if I did. It was a no brainer!

"I accept Ms. Orlov," I said to her as she smiled and nodded her head.

"Please, now that you are in my employment, you may call me Svet," she told me.

"Great, I look forward to working with you Svet and please call me June," I said as we finished our glasses of champagne and I left the hotel.

It had been four days since I agreed to close my business and work solely for Svet. It was going on five days since I met with her, but I hadn't heard from her once. It was making me nervous.

I was out shopping at the mall when the cell phone I had been given began to ring. I immediately answered the phone and said, "Hello."

"Good afternoon my unicorn. You will leave this evening for Nashville, Tennessee. A ticket will be waiting for you at the airport. Your car will arrive at 5:30 PM. Your flight leaves at 7:45 PM. You will arrive in Nashville at 12:45 PM central daylight time. Do not check any luggage. Make sure that all you require will be packed in a carryon bag. A car will retrieve you at the airport and take you to the location. Travel well and I will speak to you soon."

I left the mall, packed a carryon bag and waited for the car to arrive. As Svet had told me the car was at my apartment at 5:30 PM on the dot. As had told me, a ticket was waiting for me. As the plane took off my mind was racing. Who was I meeting with and where was I meeting?

The flight time was less than anticipated and a little past 12:30 AM central standard time I landed in Nashville. It was the first time I had ever traveled outside the state of Nevada but would be far from the last.

As Svet had told me, as I exited the terminal and made my way to the lobby there was a man in a business suit holding up a sign that read Paige Anderson. I walked to him and a short time later I was being driven but to where and to meet who I didn't know. About a half hour later it appeared that we had arrived.

It was the largest home I had ever seen in person in my life. It had to be well over 10,000 square feet and was beautiful. After going through a large security gate, the car pulled to the front of the house and came to a stop.

The driver opened my door and smiled when I exited the car.

"Ms. Anderson I will be back when you're ready to depart," he said to me.

"How do I get in contact with you?" I asked.

He smiled and said, "I'll know when to retrieve you, Ms. Anderson."

The driver entered the car as I rang the bell to the home. As the door slowly opened the driver pulled away from the front of the home and drove back down the long driveway.

What stood before me was a pretty woman, early thirties with long blond hair and light brown eyes. She was petite and had small but decent size tits. She looked oddly familiar to me, but I couldn't put my finger on where I knew her from.

"Hi, I'm Paige," I said with a smile as the nervous looking woman smiled at me and introduced herself with her first name in a sweet-sounding southern drawl.

I would, of course, like to tell you who she was, but I can't. Confidentiality is of the utmost importance and my life kind of depends on my ability to be discreet.

"Please, come in," she said to me as I entered the palatial home. The house was amazing and designed flawlessly! It wasn't until we entered the living room that who this woman became all too clear. There were music awards of all kinds as well as encased gold, silver, and platinum albums.

She was so nervous that she was shaking, and I felt that I needed to calm her down.

"You don't have anything to be nervous about," I said with an assuring voice.

"I've never done anything like this before. I was promised confidentiality" she said with her voice quivering.

"Me being here is 100% confidential. You have nothing to worry about" I replied calmly.

"If this were to get out, I would be ruined. I'm a Christian singer for God's sake" she said as her hands shook.

"Nothing is ever going to get out. I promise" I said with a smile.

"You're beautiful," she said nervously as I smiled and replied, "Thank you but so are you."

"I could use a drink. Can I get you a drink?" she asked as I nodded my head and smiled at her.

I followed her into a large room with a flat screen television, pool table, living room set and a bar that looked like it belonged in an actual bar restaurant.

"What can I get you?" she asked.

"Surprise me" I replied.

She filled two glasses with ice but as she began to pour rum into one of the glasses her hands were shaking so much, she poured more than a little onto the bar.

"Please, let me," I said calmly as I walked to the back of the bar as she took a seat at the bar directly across from me.

I fixed us the drinks and slide one across the bar to her. As she brought the glass to her lips he hand continued to tremble as she took a sip and placed the drink back onto the bar.

Her hand was resting on the table, so I placed my hand on top of hers, looked her in the eyes and said, "As I said, you have nothing to be nervous about. You don't have to do anything with me. We can just talk if you want."

She took a deep breath and exhaled. My words did calm her as I saw a smile appear on her face for the first time.

We talked and drank for hours. With each of her drinks, I could tell the effects of the alcohol brought her a sense of calm.

The more drinks she had the more open and hones she became. She confessed that she's had an attraction to women for a long time and that she felt as if she were living a lie. That due to her faith and career she felt exploring her feelings would be morally wrong but that she felt as if she were trapped in a cage.

I felt bad for her. I couldn't imagine having to hide who I was from the outside world and how I could have everything that I worked so hard for taken away over my sexuality. I fully understood how she could feel trapped by life.

When I told her how I felt about her situation she was relieved.

"It feels great to finally speak to someone about what I'm going through," she said to me with an ear to ear smile as I responded, "I'm glad I could help."

It was well past 4 AM and we had both consumed over six strongly made drinks each. I knew we were both intoxicated, especially when she seemed to completely cut loose and told me, "I'm very attracted to you."

I smiled and replied, "Well that's a good thing."

She took a deep breath and exhaled. "How does this work?" she asked.

"It's simple. You tell me what you want, and I do what you want" I said in a seductive voice.

She slowly climbed off the bar stool and took a seat on the couch that rested a few feet from the bar as I followed behind her.

I was standing in front of her when she looked at me and said, "I want to see you nude."

I smiled as I took off each of my shoes slowly. I turned around and asked, "Can you please unzip me?" I could feel her trembling hand slowly unzip my dress.

I turned myself around, so I was now facing her once again. I slid my panties off from beneath my dress slowly and seductively until I had brought them to my ankles. I stepped out my panties and proceeded to remove the straps of my dress so that the straps were now resting on my upper arms.

I unhooked my bra, removed my dress and then removed my bra. I now stood before her nude as she had wanted me.

She gazed at my nude body for a while. She looked at my body up and down over and again.

"Can I touch you?" she asked as I smiled and replied, "If that's what you want to do."

She slowly rose from the couch and closed the distance between us.

She closed her eyes as she touched my tits and slowly ran her fingers across each of my nipples. She pressed her body against mine as she reached around me and placed her hands on my ass.

She ran her face against the small of my neck and then brought her face to mine. With her eyes still closed she gently kissed my lips.

I kissed her lips back and then licked her lips with my wet tongue. I grabbed the back of her had and began to French kiss her as she kissed me back.

I was getting more and more turned on as the seconds passed. As we continued to kiss, she once again began to run her hands across my breasts and her fingers across my nipples.

I stopped kissing her and began to gently kiss her neck. I could feel her body quivering with each kiss to her neck.

I turned her around and begin to lick and nibble on her earlobe as she pressed her back into my chest. I again began to kiss her neck as unbuttoned her jeans and slowly unzipped her zipper.

I ran my right hand under the waistline of her panties and touched her pussy with two of my fingers. She was soaking wet.

As I continued to kiss and lick her neck, I began to rub her pussy as she moaned with pleasure. I then ran my left hand up her shirt and beneath her bra as I began to gently rub her nipple with my fingers. As I played with her pussy, she placed her hand over mine.

She gently took hold of my wrist and slowly pulled my hand from her pussy. She turned, faced me and gave me a nervous smile. She took my hand and walked me from the room, up the stairs, and into a large bedroom.

She laid down on the bed as I laid my nude body to the side of her. She closed her eyes as I kneeled over her and began to remove her shirt. She sat slightly up as I removed her shirt, unhooked her bra and removed it.

I laid myself on top of her so that my breasts pressed against hers as I again began to kiss her. I could feel her becoming more comfortable and less nervous as the minutes passed.

I stopped kissing her and begin to kiss her tits and gently lick her nipples. As I continued, she began to run her fingers through my hair.

I removed myself from on top of her and gently tugged on her jeans. She opened her eyes and locked onto mine as she removed her jeans and panties in one motion down to her ankles. I pulled her clothing from her legs and placed them on the floor.

I again placed my nude body on top of hers and again began to French kiss her. I stopped kissing her and worked my way down her stomach with gentle light kisses as I moved my body downward.

When I licked her pussy for the first time, she let out a short gasp and then began to moan as I licked the lips of her pussy, separated them and began to gently lick and suck on her clit.

She didn't say one single word as I continued to eat her pussy. Instead, she moaned with pleasure. I remember thinking how hot it was that she had her eyes open the entire time I ate her pussy. She wanted to watch me pleasure her and pleasure her I did until she exploded with pleasure.

This was the first time I had ever met with her, but it would be far from the last. What stands out most to me afterward was that I didn't feel sad, bad or dirty. I felt happy. I felt as if I did something for her that no one else had ever done. I brought her true self to the forefront and had a wonderful time with her at the same time.

I had only been working for Svetlana for a little over two months but had already been booked seven times. $140,000 in gross income in less than three months! I was on cloud nine. I was making more money than I could ever have imagined and was having a blast in doing so. I knew then that I could never go back to living the way I once had. There was no going back for me. The money was intoxicating. The more money I made the more money I wanted to make. The more money I needed to make.

I had been to Nashville, Seattle, San Francisco, Washington D.C., Puerto Rico, Aruba, Boston, and London! Not bad for a girl who a couple of months earlier had never left the state of Nevada. I was traveling and making a ton of money in the process.

It was a Thursday night when Svetlana called me and told me that I was heading to Malibu Beach California. She told me to pack light and that I would be in Malibu from Friday through Sunday and be on my way back home on Monday afternoon.

When I landed in Los Angeles on that Friday morning I was stunned when the same Russian man who had greeted me when I first met Svetlana did so again at the airport.

"Hello, June," he said in his heavy Russian accent as I smiled and replied, "Hello."

"Where are my manners? My name is Sergei" he said as I smiled.

"Are you my driver for this weekend?" I asked with intrigue as he laughed and replied, "I will chaperone you to Svet's home today."

Svet's home? Why was I going to her home? Had I done something wrong? Why did she feel it necessary to fly me out to her in Malibu? My mind raced as Sergei drove me to Svetlana's home.

As he pulled into the driveway, I couldn't believe what laid before me! It was the most magnificent home I had ever seen in my life. I was nervous when I exited the car and was walked into the house.

"Welcome my unicorn," Svetlana greeted me warmly as I smiled in reply.

"Please, come," she said as I followed her to the backyard of the home where I large infinity pool sat along with beautiful outdoor furniture.

"Sit, my dear," she told me as I took a deep breath, exhaled and took a seat.

"Did I do something wrong?" I asked her nervously as she smiled and then laughed.

"You have done nothing wrong, it is quite the opposite. You are doing wonderfully, and I could not be happier" she explained to me. Her words put me at ease.

"Why did you invite me here to your home?" I asked with curiosity as she smiled and answered, "It is time to relax my dear. We will be joined throughout the day by your colleagues. It is good to get to know those who do what you do for a living. It is good to relax and have fun."

As Svetlana talked to me a handsome young man joined us outside. He couldn't have been any older than twenty-four but had short cropped hair, amazing light eyes, his body was ripped to shreds complete with washboard abs.

"Marcus, come meet June," Svetlana said to him with an ear to ear smile.

"Hi June, I'm Marcus," he said as I replied, "Hi, Marcus, it's nice to meet you.'

"You two speak to one another. I must attend to matters" Svetlana said leaving us alone in the backyard.

"So, you're the new girl," he said with a smirk.

"Guess I am" I replied.

"The female unicorn," he said with laughter which made me laugh as he continued, "I'm the male unicorn."

"Male unicorn?" I asked with surprise as she nodded his head and answered, "I'm your male counterpart."

"You're gay?!" I exclaimed as he laughed and nodded his head again.

"As the sky is blue June," he said to me as I responded, "I would have never guessed. I mean, you're so, so, so…" I began to say as he cut me off mid-sentence and said, "Masculine. That's why I'm in such high demand. There are a ton of guys out there who prefer masculine gay men" as a matter of fact.

"I have a little over a handful of steady clients. A couple of NFL players, an NHL player, MLB player and a few high-powered international businessmen. That's the key to this profession. A little over a handful of steady clients and you're on easy street" he told me.

"Why are we here?" I asked naively.

"Consider this weekend an office party. You know how people who work in offices gather around the water cooler on a Monday morning so they can catch up with what happened over the weekend? Well, consider this out watercooler except we eat, drink, swim and let loose. To be honest I look forward to these weekends. There aren't many people in the world who can understand what it is we do. Welcome, you part of the family now" he said with an assuring voice.

"This is surreal. I would have never imagined I would be doing this for a living" I confessed to Marcus.

"Who would?" he asked as I shrugged my shoulders in response.

Throughout the day, more of us arrived at Svetlana's house. There was Gregory who was also gay but unlike Marcus who was nowhere near masculine. There was Tareek, an African American male escort, Dennis, a white male escort and Javier, a Cuban American escort. There was Gina, a stunning female white escort, Shantel, an African American female escort and Esmerelda, a Mexican American female escort. There was also, Matilda. Matilda was a large pretty girl, no older than twenty-two. She was beautiful and big. She wasn't fat but thick if that makes sense. Of course, there was Jane and me. In total there were eleven of us under Svetlana's employment.

Jane wasn't lying the night we had met. She was the cream of the crop, the top of the pyramid. She was the most beautiful of all us ladies and the last to arrive a bit past 7 PM.

I had found it odd when Marcus welcomed me to the family, but I no longer did when we were finally all present. It felt like a family, a real family.

People making fun of each other, cracking jokes and telling story after story of their most recent bookings. I didn't say much. I remember listening intently and laughing so much that my face hurt.

I was sitting in a chair, sipping on a drink and eating a hamburger when Jane sat next to me and said, "Keep eating like that and your figure will be gone in a heartbeat" as I shrugged my shoulders and took another bite of my hamburger.

"Is it true?" Shantel asked me which took me off guard.

"Is what true?" I asked.

She smiled and looked at Jane. "Did you make Jane cum?" she asked with her eyes wide open and an ear to ear grin.

I nodded my head in reply as everyone except for Jane burst out in laughter.

"What's so funny?" I asked with surprise.

Matilda yelled out, "Jane doesn't cum!" as everyone again burst out in laughter except for Jane.

"What?!" I exclaimed with disbelief as Jane rolled her eyes, arose from her seat and went into the house.

Javier now occupying Jane's vacant seat looked at me and said, "It's true. Our girl Jane doesn't cum. According to her, she's always faked orgasms with clients but you made her cum as witnessed by Svet. No wonder she calls you her unicorn" he laughed.

"Svet told you all about me?" I asked with a stunned tone of voice.

Tareek yelled out, "What can I say. You are indeed Svet's magical creature!" as everyone again laughed.

Esmeralda walked over to me and said, "You're not what I expected. Svet told me you were kind if introverted and a bit shy, but I don't see it."

Her words took me back. I felt different. I didn't feel like the shy introverted girl I had always been. I felt happy, confident and like I could conquer to the world.

I looked at Esmeralda and replied, "I used to be but now not so much. I think I've changed" as everyone again began to laugh.

"This job will do that to you!" Dennis yelled out.

A little over an hour later, Jane exited the house, walked over to me and said, "I need to speak to you in private."

I rose from my seat and followed her into the kitchen of the house. She was now looking at me as she leaned against the island with her arms crossed.

"I need to get something off my chest," she said to me stone-faced.

"Okay," I replied.

I knew I shouldn't be looking at her in the way that I was but couldn't help myself. She was so beautiful! Her long blond hair, her light eyes, her amazing body, her voluptuous lips, and her goddess-like face.

"What happened between you and me in Vegas was a one-time thing. Svet asked me for favor and I did the favor. That's all it, was" she said to me.

"Okay," I again said.

"Why are you looking at me that way? Stop it!" she snapped.

Perhaps it was because I had changed. Perhaps it was because I had a ton of liquid courage flowing through my veins. Thinking back, I don't recall exactly what it was, but I do recall exactly what I said.

I looked at her with lust in my eyes and replied, "I'm looking at you the way that I am because I want you."

Jane rolled her eyes and said to me with a firm tone of voice, "Look, I don't know what came over me that night, but I don't do those things. I'm straight, 100% straight as I like cock."

I giggled and replied, "Didn't stop you from putting my pussy in your mouth."

She again rolled her eyes and replied, "As I said, I don't know what came over me but be assured that it was a one-time thing and I like guys, not girls."

"Are you sure about that?" I asked seductively as she nodded her head and responded, "100% sure, June. 100% sure."

I smiled seductively at her and closed the distance between us. "You owe me," I said as a matter of fact.

"Owe you for what?!" she snapped.

"I made you cum. You owe me one orgasm at any time of your choosing" I replied.

"In your dreams," she said as she rolled her eyes yet again and shook her head.

"Reality is so much better. After all, I did make you cum" I said with a smirk.

"Fuck you, June!" she said through gritted teeth as I smiled and replied, "You promise?"

"Conversation is over. See you later" she said as she exited the kitchen and returned to the backyard.

It was a great weekend. I honestly didn't want it to come to an end. I learned so much from everyone it made my head spin. I learned so much about everyone that I felt a closeness to others I hadn't experience since my dad.

All was going great, but I had been warned. "It's not always going to be easy or pleasurable" Gina had told me that weekend. I had no idea what she was referring to but would soon find out.

It was either my tenth or eleventh booking, I can't quite remember but the encounter today is as fresh in my memory as if it had happened yesterday.

I arrived at a luxurious home in Miami, Florida and was meeting with a new client. Her name isn't important, but I had no clue as what was going to happen that night. Had I known, I would never have gone.

She was a well-known politician, a senator to be exact. A senator that publicly spoke out against the LGBT community! I recognized her immediately and couldn't believe that she had booked me.

She had this look about her that's hard to explain. It was almost as if she was disgusted by me. I knew I was disgusted by her! She was obese and had to be close to fifty years old. She was unkempt and the house was a mess.

As soon as I walked in, she walked me into her bedroom. She practically ripped my clothes off and threw me onto her bed without saying a word.

There were these straps dangling from the headboard. She tied me up with the straps and told me to get onto all fours which I did.

"You're a bad girl, a very bad girl and I'm going to punish you," she said with a tone to her voice that scared me.

I watched her go to her dresser and pull out a huge strap on. She removed her clothes and affixed the strap on.

She climbed onto the bed and with no lubricant whatsoever so proceeded to attempt to insert that huge dildo into my ass. I tried to wiggle but she grabbed me by my neck and squeezed so hard that I thought I was going to pass out.

She put a ball gag into my mouth and tied it so tight to my head I felt as if my brain would explode.

She forced the huge dildo into my ass with such force that my eyes began to water. With each thrust, the pain increased. As tears streamed from my eyes, she fucked my ass and said, "Take it like the lesbian slut you are. Take my cock, you whore bitch!"

I couldn't speak or say a word with the ball gag in my mouth. It hurt so bad I just wanted it to end. I became fixated on the alarm clock on her nightstand and watched the minutes go by as she forced the dildo in and out of my ass.

Twenty minutes! For twenty minutes she force fucked my ass until she stopped and untied one of my hand. As I rolled over, she slapped me so hard across my face that I saw stars!

She tied me up again, but I was not on my back as she again inserted the huge dildo in me. She was now fucking my pussy with the large dildo as she choked me at the same time.

"You slut bitch! Take my cock!" she exclaimed.

I thought I was going to die. I couldn't believe that this was happening to me, but it was. A little over an hour later the session was over.

"Get dressed and get the fuck out my house!" she seethed as I dressed as quickly as I could in my ripped clothes.

I ran out of the house and instead of waiting for my driver to arrive I began to walk. I felt like I was in a daze. I felt violated and as if I had just escaped from a living hell! As I walked and cried, I thought to myself, "This is over. I'm not ever doing this again!"

I managed to find my way to a hotel and rented a room for the night. I sat in the shower and cried as I had never cried before. I had to be in the shower for at around two hours. When I finally managed to get out of the shower, I wrapped myself in a towel and laid flat on my stomach on the bed.

My ass felt like it was on fire. It hurt to move so I did my best to stay still. My cell phone kept ringing, but I couldn't' bring myself to answer it.

"How could Svetlana do this to me?" was all I could think to myself over and again until I awoke in the morning with someone pounding on my hotel room door.

I managed to get my pain racked body out of bed and to the door. I slowly opened the door to find Svetlana and Sergei standing in the doorway.

"When I call you answer!" Svetlana screamed at me.

"I'm sorry...I'm..." I cried as her demeanor changed.

"My dear, what is wrong?" she asked as I told her everything that happened to me the night before.

She placed her hand on my face and said something in Russian. I didn't understand what she had told me that morning, but I now do. She said, "I'm sorry. She will never hurt you again" as she looked at Sergei with concern and anger.

I would like to tell you that this was the one and only time that this sort of thing ever happened to me, but I would be lying. These events were far and few between, but they did happen.

This was my life. This was my life for years. I was now living in Dallas, Texas after falling in love with the city while spending time with a client there. I know now the reason why I fell in love with Dallas was because of her. She was a client, the wife of a successful preacher.

I knew I was being paid to spend time with her and she knew she was paying to spend time with me, but it didn't feel that way. All I knew was that when I wasn't spending time with her, I wanted to. She reminded me of Francesca in a way. She was a mother to two young children, and she had all the money she could ever spend in three lifetimes, but she was only happy when she was with me.

When her husband was arrested and sentenced to prison for tax evasion, she felt it would be best for her to start life anew. She decided to take her children home to Italy.

It was told to me over and again, "Never develop feelings for a client," but I did. When I knew I had seen her for the last time it felt like my world had come to an end.

Everyone knew that something was wrong when we were again all together at Svetlana's home in Malibu. The only person who talked to me about it was Jane.

Jane and I had become close over the years as did Marcus and I. Marcus was the brother I never had. Jane was the woman I wanted but couldn't have. I had decided that it was in my best interest to have her as a friend as opposed to not at all.

If it weren't for Jane and Marcus, I don't think I would have ever gotten over her. Jane was my rock and Marcus was my emotional soul mate. He too was going through what I was. He was madly in love with a professional baseball player but knew it could never be more than what it was.

I was Svet's unicorn, but Jane was mine. I looked forward to seeing her and when I did it was bittersweet. I loved seeing her, but it hurt that I wanted her, and she didn't want me. I was infatuated with her and it was becoming worse until one-day things changed in a way I could have never imagined.

I decided that I would take a long overdue vacation to New York City. Svet more than agreed it was time for me to take a break and gave me three months off. It was a place I had been to less than a handful of times, but I loved it. It was fast paced, and it there was a countless number of musicals I wanted to see.

I decided to spoil myself at booked a suite at the Saint Regis for my entire time in New York City. I could care less that I was going to spend over $100,000 on hotel accommodations. It wouldn't even put a dent into my savings account!

I had only been in New York City for a little less than a week but had seen Wicked, Rent, and Les Misérables. I was having the time of my life! I don't recall the exact night, but the night happened.

I decided I wanted to have a few drinks and found a place not too far from my hotel. It was well after 11 PM as I sat at the bar. I needed to pee badly so I rose from my seat at the bar and as I began to walk to the bathroom, I heard a voice I never thought I would ever hear again.

"Oh my God! June! June! June!" the familiar voice yelled out.

I whipped my head around and there she was, Danielle.

It felt like I was having an out of body experience as I watched Danielle move through the crowded bar and in my direction. She now stood before me.

"Danielle? Danielle? Is it really you?" I asked with shock.

"June! I can't believe it!" she screamed out as she hugged me tightly.

Her embrace felt amazing. She looked the same but a bit different. She looked like she had always except for a pair of thin glasses that now rested on her face.

"What the fuck are you doing here?" she asked as I smiled and replied, "I'm on vacation."

"Where are you going?" she asked as I smiled and replied, "The little girls, room."

"I'll keep your seat warm. Hurry the fuck up!" she yelled out.

It felt like the line to the bathroom was eternal. I was beyond intoxicated and my heart felt like it was about to leave my chest. Danielle! Danielle was sitting in my bar stool waiting for me!

I nervously walked back to the bar. When she looked at me and smiled all that I had ever felt for her came rushing back as if it had been held by a damn for all these years

She was so excited to see me that she was bouncing up and down on the bar stool with an ear to ear smile.

All I could say to myself was "Be cool." "So, what are you doing here?" I asked.

"I decided to have a few after work cocktails. I'm working for a small architectural firm close by and working on my masters" she said to me.

"That's great!" I exclaimed as she ordered four shots.

"What are you doing with yourself?" she asks with her eyes wide open.

"I'm a headhunter. My firm is in Los Angeles and I haven't taken a vacation since I started so they told me to take three months off and told me I didn't have a choice" I lied.

"Three months? Wow, impressive. You must be good" she said to me.

"The best" I responded with a smile.

"Where are you staying?" she asked as I smiled and replied, "The Saint Regis."

"You must be the best to be able to stay at the Saint Regis for three fucking months!" she yelled out as she slid a shot to me.

We drank the shots and talked for a while. It was as if the time we spent apart didn't matter. It felt natural to speak to her as if we had parted ways days ago.

It wasn't until a little after 1 AM when a handsome man made his way toward us.

"Baby!" the man exclaimed as Danielle whipped her head around and looked at the man.

"June, this is my fiancé, Craig!" she exclaimed as she kissed him and introduced us.

"June? Nice to meet you" he said with a tone of voice that said the opposite of nice to meet you.

"You're drunk and we should go," he said to her as she shook her head and replied, "I'm hanging with June."

"I know you are but it's late. I'll take you home" he said to her.

"Give me your fucking number now!" she yelled out with laughter as I entered my cell phone number into her cell phone.

"You and I are hanging out!" she yelled out as she laughed, hugged me and kissed me on my cheek.

"Of course," I replied with a smile as I watched Craig walk her out of the bar.

I paid the tab and walked out into the hot summer night.

As I walked back to my hotel, I felt upset. She was engaged to be married? She was getting married to a guy named Craig? Why didn't I notice her engagement ring?

No matter how much time had passed I had always thought about her and as if by destiny Danielle as if hearing my thoughts had found me. Maybe we had found each other? All I knew was that I needed to see her again.

When I awoke in the morning, I awoke to a text from Danielle that read, "Me and you, Friday night!"

I replied, "Meet me at my hotel!"

I felt like an eternity waiting for that Friday night to arrive. When Danielle arrived at my hotel room she was in complete and utter amazement.

"This place is amazing," she said to me in a low tone of voice.

"Yeah, I guess it is" I replied.

"What do you want to do?" I asked her.

"We should just hang here. We should have a few drinks and catch up" she said with a smile.

"Sounds like a plan" I smiled in reply.

It had been years since we had seen each other yet it felt like no time had passed at all. We ordered room service and enjoyed cocktails and each other's company until the sun set and rose again.

She was still at Columbia but now studying for her master's degree in architecture. She told me that she met Craig during her junior year in college at a club in the city and that they hit it off right away.

She told me that she and Craig had set a date for July of the following year. She told me that Craig was an international corporate lawyer specializing in acquisitions and mergers and even though they spent more time apart than together that she was happy.

I don't know if it was that I didn't want to believe that she happy didn't believe her when said the words to me, but I didn't feel that she was happy. Years had passed but I still knew her facial expressions and her tones of voice.

I told her all about my time with Francesca and how it ended. I told her about my massage business, leaving out the erotic massage part and lied to her when I told her that a massage client recommended me to the recruitment firm as he worked for the same company in management.

She wasn't lying when she told me that she and Craig spent more time apart than together. For a little over a month, he was rarely home, and I found Danielle and I got to together more frequently. We spent at least three nights per week hanging out and every weekend.

The more time we spent together the more those feelings I once had for her strengthened. We were hanging out at my hotel room on a Saturday night after enjoying dinner and a musical.

I could tell that there was something on her mind, but I couldn't put my finger on exactly what it was.

"June, I need to apologize to you," she said to me.

"About what?" I asked.

"I'm sorry that we lost touch. It was entirely my fault" she said.

"I don't think so. I think we just naturally drifted apart. I was in Nevada and you were here in New York City" I replied.

She shook her head and gazed into my eyes. "No, it was my fault. The day I said goodbye to you was the worst day of my life. I missed you so much. When we spoke on the phone it was too much for me to bear. I can't describe the pain I felt" she explained.

"It's okay," I said with an assuring voice.

"No, it's not. If I could go back in time, I would change things. I would have told you that I loved you and that I needed you to be with me. I would have stayed in Nevada if you had asked me" she said with tears in her eyes.

"I didn't ask. I wanted to but I knew that I was heading nowhere and couldn't bear the thought of ruining your life. Anyway, things worked out well for both of us" I replied with a smile.

"June, this is going to sound crazy. I knew it is but since you've come back into my life, I've been as happy as I've been in a long time. I know I'm engaged, and I have a wedding date but everything in my mind and body tell me that you're the person I should be with" she said full of emotion.

"Danielle, I'm not the same person that I was. I've changed" I said with tears filling my eyes.

"I've changed too. I knew we're not teenagers anymore and when people age, they change but I know you. You're still that person I fell in love with. If I'm wrong, just tell me. You loved me too" she said to me.

I nodded my head and replied, "Yeah I did love you and I would be lying if I said that those feelings haven't come back."

She smiled and then kissed me. Her lips again touching mine felt so right. As we French kissed and caressed each other's bodies I had never wanted anyone so bad before.

As I laid my body on top of hers on the couch it was if I was struck by a bolt of lightning. She was engaged to be married and I was an escort. Being an escort was my profession. How could I possibly start a relationship again with Danielle? If I told her what it was, I did for a living she would leave so what would be the point?

I removed myself from her and stood up.

"What's wrong?" she asked with surprise.

"This is wrong, and it shouldn't happen. You're engaged and getting married next summer" I told her.

"I know I am, but I want you. I want you June! I'll leave him for you!" she exclaimed.

"This is not what you want, believe me," I replied.

"I'm a grown woman and I know what I want. What I want is you!" she yelled out.

"No, I can't. Some things are best left in the past" I said to her.

"You just told me that those feeling you had for me is still here! I'm throwing myself at you! I told you that I want you. I told you I would leave Craig for you! What is the problem here?!" she screeched.

"I'm not the same person anymore Danielle!" I yelled back.

She fixed her shirt, ran her fingers through her hair and sat up on the couch. She rose to her feet and looked at me with disbelief.

"There's a reason why I walked into that bar that night. It was destiny. It was meant for you to come back into my life. I've never been happier" she said to me with passion.

"Danielle, no," I said to her.

"No? Why the fuck not?!" she vented.

"It's only been a little over a month," I said to her.

"You have no clue! No clue what it was like for me! Not a day or night has passed without me thinking about you! You are the love of my life and now we're here, together again! How could you just say no to me?!" she yelled out in pain.

"You wouldn't understand!" I yelled out.

"I wouldn't understand?! What? Fucking, try me!" she screamed out.

"I'm not a recruiter! I'm a high-end escort!" I yelled back without thinking for a second.

The silence between us was deafening.

"You're a prostitute?" she asked with tears streaming from her eyes.

"No, I'm a high-end escort. Women pay to spend time with me" I replied.

"What do you do during this time?" she asked dumbfounded.

"Whatever they want to do" I quickly replied.

"Sexually?" she asked shaking her head.

"Yeah" I confessed.

"How long has it been?" she asked with her face now taking on a pale tone.

"Years" was how I responded.

"Years" she repeated. "How many women have you been with over the years?" she asked.

"A lot" I replied.

"You have sex with women for money. Selling your body for sex is the very definition of prostitution!" she snapped as she placed her hands over her mouth.

"You don't know what my life was like. I was almost homeless. If it weren't for Francesca I would have been. I became a licensed masseuse and just kind of fell into the profession" I tried to explain.

"Profession? Becoming a doctor is a profession. Becoming a lawyer is a profession. Becoming an architect is a profession. Hell, being a corporate recruiter is a profession. Fucking women for money is not a profession, it's what a whore does!" she said with anger.

"You're judging me?" I asked in horror.

"Sorry, I know how much you've always hated that but yeah, how can I not? I told you I wanted to be with you, and you told me you're a prostitute" she said with a look of sickness.

"I guess this changes things, huh?" I asked.

"I would say so" she confessed.

"What was I supposed to do?" I asked her.

"You could have gone to college. You could have taken a shitty paying job and lived just above broke like most people in this fucking world. Instead, you decided to sell your body for money" she said with disgust.

"If I could have, I would have!" I screamed out.

"You're right, you're not the same person you once were. You're fucking pathetic but thank you. Thank you for being honest with me and not letting me make a huge fucking mistake!" she screamed out.

Her words were like a dagger to my heart.

"It was destiny that I walked into that bar that night. I've been holding onto to something that I shouldn't have been. I have closure now so you're right, no" she said coldly.

"So, this is it then?" I asked as tears streamed from my eyes.

She nodded her head and looked at me with daggers in her eyes. "Goodbye, June," she said as she grabbed her purse, opened the door and slammed it hard behind her. It would be the last time I ever saw or heard from her.

I the morning I checked out of the hotel, rented a car and began to drive. I didn't know where I was going but knew I needed to leave New York. I found myself driving back home to Dallas but when I entered Maryland I decided to head into Baltimore. For the next week, I drove on the route back to Dallas but made stops along the way.

As the days passed, I realized I couldn't be angry at Danielle for reacting the way she did. Deep down I knew that she was going to react the way she did, but it did hurt.

I found myself in Kentucky when Jane called me.

"What up bitch?" she asked with laughter.

"Heading home" I replied somberly.

"I thought you were vacationing in NYC?" she replied.

"I was but I ran into Danielle and long story short I'm heading home now" I answered.

"Danielle as in Danielle, Danielle?" she asked in a high-pitched tone of voice.

"Yeah, Danielle, Danielle" I replied and proceeded to tell Jane all that had happened during my time in New York City.

"Wow, that's fucking insane! Anyway, since you're still on vacation and I'm on vacation, you need to bring that ass to Chicago!" she yelled out.

"What's in Chicago?" I asked without thinking.

"Me, bitch. I want to hang out so put my address into your GPS and come hang with your girl" she said.

I thought for a moment and decided why not?

"On my way" I replied as I entered her address into my GPS. I was now on my way to see Jane at her home in Chicago.

A little under nine hours later I arrived at Jane's luxury apartment in Old Town, Chicago. It was well after 10 PM and I was exhausted.

Jane looked at me and smiled as I entered her expensive one-bedroom apartment.

"You look like shit" she laughed as I replied, "I feel like shit but thanks."

She handed me a beer as I took a seat in her living room and drank the entire beer in one swig. I burped and said, "Keep them coming."

"I have something way better," she said with a smirk.

"What would that be?" I asked with intrigue.

"Killer fucking weed. I mean this shit is insane" she said with a smirk as I shrugged my shoulders.

As she rolled a couple of joints, she smiled at me and said, "Thanks for coming over" as I replied, "Thanks for the invite."

We lit our joints and began to smoke.

"I'm sorry about Danielle, I know how much she meant to you but a relationship with a normal is not in our cards," she said to me.

"A normal? Really?" I replied as I took a drag from my joint and rolled my eyes.

She laughed and answered, "Face the facts. We do what we do for a living because we're fucked up individuals. No one in their right mind would choose to do what we do and deal with what we deal with. What type of normal person would ever want to be with people like us?"

"I never really thought about it," I said to her in reply.

"Why do you do it?" she asked.

"The money" I responded with laughter.

"The money is so great!" she laughed out loud.

"So, this is it? This is what our lives are? We fuck for money. Then what?" I asked philosophically.

"Thailand" she replied.

"Thailand? What about Thailand?" I asked with amusement.

"When it's all said and done, I'm going to live in Thailand," she said with an ear to ear smile.

"Why Thailand?" I asked.

"It's paradise, a very cheap paradise. I could live like a queen on a $1,000 a month. Considering I'm U.S. rich I could live like a fucking billionaire there" she replied with a wink.

"When is it all said and done?" I asked as she shrugged her shoulders.

She then smiled at me and said in reply, "When it's time."

"When will that be?" I asked.

"When it's time" she replied shaking her head and looking at me as if I were crazy.

I let out a sigh in response.

"June, stop it. What happened between you and Danielle is for the best" she said with conviction.

"I know it is, but it still sucks. I mean if I did anything else for a living, things would have been different" I said to her.

She took a huge drag of her joint, held it in for a moment and exhaled with a huge smile on her face.

"If you did anything else for a living you wouldn't have been in New York when you were. You wouldn't have bumped into her. There's a reason why things happen the way they do even though we don't always understand why. At some point in time, we all wind up exactly where we should be and where we want to be. Life is just easier for some than it is for others" she explained to me.

At this point, I had only taken a few drags from my joint, but I was high as a kite.

"For all the time we've known each other you know everything about me, but I barely know anything about you," I said to Jane.

"What would you like to know?" she asked me.

"Why did you get into our line of work?" I asked really wanting to know.

She took another drag from her joint and looked at me.

"You really want to know?" she asked as I slowly nodded my head.

"I figured I was damaged goods already so why not get into this line of work. It's not like I would ever be able to have a normal relationship, especially after what I went through. I guess I felt it was a natural fit" she said to me.

"What did you go through?" I asked with intrigue.

She looked at me in a way she had never looked at me before. She took a deep breath, exhaled and sighed.

"Fuck it, we're friends and I trust you. I was sexually abused by my stepfather for as long as I could remember. I thought for a long time he was my biological father but by the time I got into junior high school I knew what he was doing to me was wrong. I didn't know any better, I thought it was a normal father, daughter relationship. When I was in eighth grade I ran away from home and here I am" she said with sadness.

"Oh my God. Did you leave home in the eighth grade? How old were you?" I asked with sadness and concern.

"Thirteen" she replied.

"Your mom didn't try to find you?" I asked.

"My mom? Fuck her! She knew what was happening, but she didn't do a thing about it. As long as he kept giving her money to inject into her veins, she was all good" she told me with anger.

I was stunned and not quite sure what to say.

"I'm so sorry," I said with tears forming in my eyes.

"Thanks, but you had nothing to do with it," she said with a head nod.

"Where did you live? What did you do?" I asked as if having diarrhea of the mouth.

"I lived on the streets for a long time and sold my body the same as I do now. I just make a hell of a lot more money doing it now" she said with no emotion.

"But you were so young," I said with exasperation.

"You'd be surprised how many perverts out there are willing to part with green pieces of paper for a piece of young pussy," she said with a smirk.

"You don't enjoy bookings, do you? Is that why you don't cum?" I asked.

She laughed so hard that she started to tear. She looked at me and smiled as she said, "I do cum, just not very often. It depends on the client. I will say that my getting off is far and few between. I've become quite the expert at faking it though" again with laughter.

"Did you fake it with me?" I asked with a seductive voice.

Jane shook her head and replied, "Nope, you got me off. That's one of the reasons you are Svet's unicorn."

The conversation felt too serious and I felt I needed to change the subject a bit. However, as if I wasn't in control of my own brain I smiled and said, "You know you still owe me."

She again laughed so hard she began to tear.

"June, I don't owe you shit. Svet paid me, you got me off and you got the job because of it. That's all" she said with a wink.

We finished our joints, got the munchies, watched Comedy Central and both fell asleep on her couch in the living room.

Spending time with Jane was great but as always, the more time I spent with her the more difficult it became for me. I had never felt such a strong attraction to another person in my life!

We went to the movies, hit a few clubs, went out shopping, went out to eat and went for long walks when we just talked about anything and everything.

When I found myself spending time with Jane at her home the longest, I could ever last was a few days but here I was closing in on a week and I couldn't take much more. It didn't help that we always shared a bed.

I could barely sleep and was lucky to get a few quality hours in. In the morning I decided it would be best for me to head home to Dallas.

I took a long hot shower, wrapped myself in a towel and began to pack my things as Jane entered the shower immediately after I vacated the bathroom.

"Where are you going?" she asked as I zipped up my bag.

"Time for me to head on home" I replied.

"Why?" she asked me.

"I haven't been home in a while and I miss it so I'm heading out" I smiled in response as I began to get dressed.

"We have close to two months more off. You were going to spend your entire vacation in New York City so why leave now?" she said with a tinge of anger present in her voice.

"It's just time for me to go is all" I responded with an eye roll.

"You always do this! We have a great time and then out of nowhere, you decide it's time to leave. Why can't you spend more time with me? Why is it that you always leave almost as soon as you get here?!" she exclaimed.

"I don't always" I replied knowing full well she was right.

"Aren't we friends?" she asked with concern.

"Of course, we are" I instantly replied.

"Great! I'll pack a bag and I'll head down to Dallas with you" she told me with a smirk.

"I didn't invite you to my home, Jane" I responded.

"Invite me then!" she vented.

"I have to go" I replied.

"We're supposed to be friends. I invite you over all the time, but not once, not once have you ever invited me to your place. Not once, June, why?"

"I have my reasons!" I seethed.

"Reasons? I know the real reason. We're allegedly friends but you can only stand to be around me for so long. Be honest, you can only take me in small doses" she said becoming increasingly upset.

"No! That's not it at all. I love spending time with you!" I exclaimed.

"So, what is it?! Why do you want to leave now?! Just be honest with me!" she screamed out.

Without thinking for a second a screamed out, "Because I have to! I can't take this!"

My words took her back. She looked at me with her beautiful tear-filled eyes and asked, "What can't you take?"

"You! Okay, you! I love spending time with you but you're my unicorn. You are the magical creature that is forever out of my reach!" I screamed out.

She smiled and replied, "Thank you for being honest," she said in a low voice.

The words that followed came from my mouth as if my words were lava flowing from a volcano that erupted.

"I'll admit it! The first time I ever saw you it was pure lust. You're the most beautiful girl I've ever laid eyes on. When you ate my pussy that night it was the greatest feeling of my life. The hottest girl I had ever laid eyes on, a straight girl, was so turned on by me that she ate my pussy. I have an orgasm to the girl who normally doesn't have orgasms. My feelings of lust turned into something else over time. You're so strong, so confident, beautiful and you know me better than anyone else on this planet!" I exclaimed with passion.

She looked at me and said, "Danielle."

I lost it! "Danielle?! Danielle?! Danielle is disgusted by me and I'm okay with that! The only reason I'm okay with it is because of you. I was devastated over what Danielle said to me but one day, one day with you and it didn't matter. It doesn't matter!" I screamed at the top of my lungs.

What happened next was not what I would have ever expected. Jane looked at me and began to cry hysterically. She placed her hands over her face and cried into her hands with her entire body shaking.

"I'm so sorry. I didn't want this. I get it, you're straight and I'm gay and what I want can never happen. I get it, but it doesn't change my feelings. I must go. I must go for my sanity. You're not attracted to me, I get it, but I need you to understand how hard it can be for me to be around you" I cried out with passion.

"Who the fuck said I'm not attracted to you?!" she yelled with such fury that it almost frightened me.

"You're attracted to me?" I asked her with my heart feeling as if it were about to explode from my chest.

"You're beautiful and such a good person. I've always had trouble developing and maintaining friendships but with you it's different. The night we first me I was so confused. I had not once thought of being with a girl but when I looked at you that night, I was extremely attracted to you. Deep down inside I knew I wanted you. It scared me. After we did what we did I felt different. That night changed me. Spending time with you changed me" she confessed.

"How?" I asked with my heart continuing to pound and my body beginning to perspire.

"I've only been attracted to one girl and one girl only in my entire life. That girl is you June and always has been" she said with a trembling voice.

I had imagined hearing those words come from her mouth but hearing them was so much better than I could have ever hoped for.

She exhaled deeply and said, "If it were possible for me to be in a relationship, I would with you but it's not a good idea" she attempted to explain.

"Starting a relationship is not impossible, Jane," I said shaking my head.

"June, first and foremost we're friends. Second, we do what we do for a living. If we were to become involved it would only end in disaster. Being faithful is not an option" she said with a serious tone.

"Sex is our business. If we were to get involved, I could handle you being with clients. It's just business" I replied with hope.

"I'm glad that you could handle it, but I don't know if I could" she explained.

"So why not find out, Jane?" I asked. I thought for a moment and asked, "Is this your way of letting me down easy?" trying unsuccessfully to prevent myself from becoming upset.

"I've thought long and hard about this. I'm not blind, June. I've seen the way you look at me, the way you've always looked at me and I know what I feel for you is something more than just friendship" she said with conviction.

She looked at me with sadness and said, "Trust me, the worst thing we could possibly do is to become involved."

"So, what do we do?" I asked with fading hope.

"What we've always done. We stay friends and whatever feelings we have toward one another we don't' act on" she said with a smile.

"Friends? Don't act on our feelings?" I said with tears streaming from my eyes.

It was as if I was hit in my heart with a dagger. I had wanted to be with her for so long but never thought it could happen. Instead, she told me that she's attracted to me, that what she feels toward me is something more than friendship, but we can't become involved. At that moment I wished I would have just left and not had the conversation with her.

"I need to go," I said as she looked at me and shook her head.

"Please don't," she said to me.

I grabbed my bag, exited the bedroom and as I walked to her front door, she ran passed me and placed her body across it, blocking me from exiting her apartment.

"Jane, please move. Please let me leave" I said crying.

"I don't want you to leave like this. Tell me we're okay" she pleaded.

"We're okay," I said lying through my teeth.

"I don't believe you. Promise me that we're okay" she again pleaded.

"I can't promise you. I'm sorry but we can't do this anymore. If we can't act on our feelings, there's only one logical thing to do. We need to stay away from each other. We need to stay away from each other for as long as whatever we both feels goes away" I told her through tears.

"Please don't cry," she said to me with concern as she removed her body from the door and embraced me tightly.

I pulled away from her as I continued to cry. "Jane, no more texting, no more speaking on the phone for hours on end. No more Face Time or Skype. We need to stay away from each other from here on out for as long as it takes," I said with my voice cracking and tears pouring out of my eyes.

She shook her head, wiped the tears from my eyes and gazed into them. Then what I had always wanted happened. What I had always dreamed about happened. She kissed me. It wasn't just that she kissed me, it was how she kissed me. She kissed me with a passion that I had never experienced before.

I pulled away from her and said, "You did that because that's what you thought I wanted" I said to her.

She shook her head and responded, "I did that because I wanted to and I know you wanted me to."

Her words brought a smile to my face.

"What did you think?" I asked with hope.

"It was nice" she smiled as she again kissed me.

Within seconds we were French kissing in her living room with our hands feeling each other's bodies.

Suddenly she pulled away from me and said, "I'm sorry. I shouldn't have done that, and we shouldn't be doing this."

"Jane! You are confusing the shit out of me!" I yelled and she yelled back, "I know!"

"This is simple. You either want me or you don't. Just be honest with me damn it!" I screamed out.

She didn't reply. She just stood there looking at me and then closed her eyes tightly.

"I'm going home," I said with an upset voice. I walked to her front door but just as I was about to open the door, she placed her hand on my shoulder.

I turned to face her when she suddenly pushed me against the door and pressed her body against mine. She again kissed me with such passion I felt as if my knees were going to give out.

As we again French kissed, I could feel myself becoming wet. We were making out for a while when I felt her hand begin to caress my lower stomach. I heard the button on my shorts become undone and the shorts become loose around my waist.

I felt her hand go beneath my panties. When she touched my pussy, I felt like I wanted to faint.

I had wanted something, anything to happen between Jane and me for so long but now that it was happening it didn't feel real.

However, when I felt her fingers being to rub my clit, I knew what was happening was indeed a reality. There I was with her tongue in my mouth, with her body pressed against mine and with her hand playing with my pussy.

I don't remember exactly how long she played with me, but I remember I stopped kissing her, wrapped my arms around her neck, gazed into her beautiful eyes and had an intense orgasm.

I came so hard that my knees gave out. Thankfully when they did Jane held onto me to prevent me from falling. I was breathing so hard I could barely catch my breath.

She was looking at me the way I had always wanted her to look at me. I became completely lost in the moment. When I kissed her my entire body became engulfed with a tingling sensation.

It was as if we were speaking to each other without saying a word. Our eyes and body language said everything that needed to be said.

What followed was over two hours of the most amazing sex of my life! For as many women that I had sex with I never felt anything close to what I felt that day. I felt so connected to her. Every one of her touches of my body made me feel vulnerable and excited at the same time.

I ate her pussy until she orgasmed but didn't stop when she did. Instead, I kept eating her pussy and fingering her pussy until she came for a second time.

When she went down on me it was as if she had done this before. I knew the only time she had ever tasted pussy was my pussy the day she ate for a little while when I made her cum in front of Svetlana those years ago. However, she ate my pussy as if she were a fucking pro!

After she made me cum, she placed her arms on my legs and looked up at me.

I smiled and asked, "How do I taste?"

She smiled and let out a giggle as she replied, "Sweet with a hint of saltiness."

"Did you enjoy doing that to me?" I asked.

She nodded her head, licked her lips and proceeded to go down on me again. When she made me cum yet again my body felt like putty.

After that, I dominated her like I never had dominated a girl before. I couldn't get enough of her taste and when I made her cum by tongue fucking her ass as I played with her clit, I felt like I had just climbed Mt. Everest. I loved every squirm of her body and every moan that came from her mouth.

When it was over, we both laid in her bed, panting like wild dogs and sweating as though we had finished running a marathon.

That day was such an emotional roller coaster and physically taxing that I was beyond exhausted. I remember cuddling against her, feeling a sense of peace and falling asleep with joy. I remember momentarily opening my drowsy eyes to see Jane with her eyes closed and a huge smile on her face.

When I awoke the next morning, Jane wasn't in bed. I could hear her arguing loudly on her cell phone through the open door of her bedroom.

"I know but she needs me!" I heard her yell out. There was a moment of silence and then I heard her say, "Thank you so much."

She walked into her bedroom and smiled at me.

"We have a whole other month off" she winked.

"What? How? Why?" I asked with confusion.

I had a long conversation with Svet. I told her about your ordeal with Danielle and how mentally distraught you are. I told her that you needed me and that Svet needed me to get you back into your right frame of mind as you're a complete disaster. She was more than reluctant but she gave us more time off to help you of course" she explained to me with laughter.

We spent a few more days in Chicago, going out to clubs, enjoying each other's bodies and company. I was in a state of complete and utter bliss.

We had spent a quiet night in watching movies the night before. When I awoke, I heard her singing along to a song as she showered.

She exited the bathroom nude, jumped on top of me and gently kissed my lips.

"Will you go somewhere with me?" she asked.

"Where?" I asked with curiosity.

"I have a small cabin in Mackinaw City, Michigan right off Douglas Lake. It's not much but it's great. It's my special place and I want you to experience it with me. Will you come with me?" she asked with a smile.

"Yeah, it sounds great" I replied with a smile.

I showered, we ate a small breakfast and then I went shopping for a few items. When I returned to her apartment, we made the over 6-hour drive from Chicago to Mackinaw City.

Jane had told me it wasn't much, and it wasn't but I loved it immediately. It was a small wood cabin with a small bedroom, and a tiny kitchen, a tiny bathroom with a decent sized living room. It had a rustic feel to it and thankfully there was internet access so we could stream movies and music.

I never had someone completely open-up to me before but that week in her cabin was what she did. It made me feel special and even more connected to her.

My heart leaped for joy when she said, "I had been so confused over my sexuality but I'm not anymore. Thank you."

She was so affectionate toward me. I had never been so happy in my life. That week we fucked each other's brains out, laughed, cried, went on walks, hikes, bike rides and for swims. It was serenity drinking wine late at night around a small fire as we sat talking and looking out to the lake.

It was during one of our final nights at the cabin. Jane was uncharacteristically quiet as I shopped for clothes and shoes online.

"You're quiet tonight," I said to her as she flashed a quick smile.

"Is something on your mind?" I asked with concern as she again flashed a quick smile.

I knew something was on her mind, but she seemed as if she were unsure about how to bring up whatever she wanted to talk to me about.

I let out a laugh, closed the lid to my laptop and placed it on the seat next to me. I looked at her and said, "Spit it out."

"I don't want to make you upset," she said with hesitation.

My heart sank momentarily as I looked at her.

"What is it? Are you having second thoughts about us?" I asked trying to prevent myself from panicking.

She shook her head and replied, "No, this is great. It's better than I thought it could be. It's just...just...just that...I..." she stumbled over her words.

What was happening? She was having second thoughts about us? Was she about to tell me that we can't be together anymore?

My body began to tremble as I looked at her with concern.

"Jane, just please tell me what's on your mind," I said to her.

She took a deep breath, slowly exhaled and looked at me with a pained looked on her face.

"What we have going is great. I'm so happy but, I..., um...I..." she again stumbled over her words and I looked at her and said, "Just tell me."

"I kind of miss cock" she confessed.

"You miss cock?" I replied as I began to laugh so hard that I began to tear.

"It's not funny, June. You've never had a cock, so you don't have a clue" she replied with an eye roll.

"I've never had a real cock, but I do have something I've been told is as close to the real thing as it gets" I responded to her.

She looked at me and laughed as she said, "Go on."

"Give me a second," I said to her as I went into the bedroom, into my bag and pulled out the new strap on I had purchased back in Chicago before we left.

I excitedly entered the living with the strap on in hand and handed it to her.

"Wow, this feels so fucking real," she said to me with amazement as she touched the dildo, pulled on it and slapped it in her hand.

"That is the best and most expensive dildo on the market and my weapon of choice out in the field," I said to her with a grin.

"Want to try it out?" I asked seductively as she looked at me and nodded her head with excitement.

I kissed her as I slowly undressed her. Once she was nude, I walked her over to the small circular wooden table and bent her over it. I removed my clothes, affixed the strap on and ate her pussy from behind as she moaned with pleasure.

Once she was soaking wet, I gently inserted the dildo into her pussy as she let out a gasp of pleasure. I slowly began to thrust as she moaned, "Oh God, that feels so good."

I was fucking her at a slow and steady pace as she yelled out, "Faster, please go faster" as I did what she asked.

"Harder, fuck me harder!" she exclaimed as I found myself pounding her from behind.

"Pull my hair!" she yelled out to me as I grabbed a fist full of hair and jerked her head back. I was now pounding her pussy as hard as I could with a fist full of her hair wrapped in my right hand as I leaned over her with my tits pressed against her back.

"Fuck! Oh God...yes...just like that, don't stop...shit...fuck...yes...oh God!" she screamed out.

Her entire body began to shake violently as she began to thrust herself harder and harder into me as I fucked her.

Her arms were locked straight as she gripped the table directly in front of her as I continued to fuck her as hard as I could as I jerked her head back violently.

I had never heard anyone cum as hard as she did! She screamed out so loud it was almost ear piercing. As she orgasmed, her arms folded as her torso crashed onto the table violently and with a thud.

I slowly removed the dildo from her pussy and kissed her back and neck.

Her breathing was beyond erratic as she struggled to catch her breath.

"Help me up," she said in a low and exhausted voice as I took hold of her hand and pulled her off the table.

She had a look of pure pleasure on her face as she kissed me and said, "That was fucking amazing. When I felt your tits press against my back as you fucked me, I thought I was going to lose my mind" she said to me.

"I thought you did lose your mind," I said jokingly as she laughed and replied, "Maybe just a little bit."

"Was that as good as the real thing?" I asked as she smiled and shook her head.

"No, it was so much better," she said with a serious look on her face.

She couldn't get enough of it, but it didn't bother me. I've experienced the feeling of that dildo and although I didn't and still don't know what it's like to be fucked by a real cock, I do know how great it felt each time I was fucked with it.

We had initially decided that we would go back to her apartment in Old Town, but I missed Dallas.

"Jane, come home with me," I said to her that morning as we put our things into her car.

"You're finally inviting me to your home? It's so sudden" she laughed as I rolled my eyes and asked, "Will you come home with me?"

She smiled and replied, "Yeah but it's a long drive. Why don't we fly to your house from Chicago?"

"We could but then it wouldn't be a road trip" I replied with a smile.

We drove from the cabin to her apartment in Chicago so we could wash our clothes and she could pack a few bags. We spent the night in her apartment and the next morning began the over 17-hour drive to my apartment in Dallas.

We made a few stops along the way and decided to stay at a hotel when we were about five hours away from Dallas. We arrived at my apartment a little past 1 PM on the following day.

We had only been at my place for a couple of days when my cell phone went off with a reminder message. I looked at the reminder that read, "Marcus, Miami."

I looked at Jane with my eyes as big as a deer in headlights.

"Shit, Marcus' birthday bash in Miami is tomorrow night" as Jane shrugged her shoulders and replied, "Yeah, I know."

"How in the hell are we getting there for tomorrow?" I asked as she shook her head and said, "I purchased tickets a few days ago."

That night we were Miami bound. I was super excited to see Marcus. We hadn't been able to talk much, and I missed him badly.

As we entered the lobby to Marcus' rented high rise condominium, we bumped into Gina and Shantel who were talking to one another.

"Bitches!" Jane exclaimed as we all hugged and greeted each other.

"Before we go up to Marcus' let's get a few cocktails in so we can catch up," Gina said as Jane and Shantel agreed.

"I want to see Marcus asap, so you bitches enjoy," I said as they left the lobby and the concierge escorted me to Marcus's unit with our bags.

As soon as the concierge and I exited the elevator there was Marcus with a huge smile on his face.

He ran over to me, hugged me tightly, lifted me in the air and kissed me on my cheek.

"I missed you so much!" he exclaimed as I giggled and replied, "Likewise boy toy."

I told him that Jane and I bumped into Gina and Shantel in the lobby and that they went for a few drinks as he smiled at me.

We entered his unit and walked out to his balcony that had an amazing few of downtown Miami. He opened a bottle of wine, poured two glasses and handed me a glass.

I couldn't help but notice the way he was looking at me.

"Marcus, what?" I asked him as he smiled at me and replied, "You look different."

I laughed and responded, "How so?" as he looked at my face and said, "You have a glow about you."

I shrugged my shoulders and took a sip of my wine as Marcus and I talked for close to two hours before party guests began to trickle in. The party was well underway when Jane, Shantel, and Gina finally arrived at Marcus'.

The party was insane! He had a DJ that was playing Techno and Trance music while people popped pills and snorted cocaine as they danced and drank.

I was buzzed working on drunk as I danced with Marcus. Out of the corner of my eye, I watched a handsome young guy approach Jane and hand her a drink. She took the drink from his hand, smiled and clinked glasses with the guy as he talked to her as she laughed.

As I danced with Marcus, I became fixated on Jane and the guy she was talking to. What was it I was feeling at this moment? I had never experienced this feeling before and I couldn't quite put my finger on what was bothering me. I now know very well the feeling I was experiencing. It was jealousy!

I stopped dancing and made a beeline to Jane. She locked onto me as I walked across the room and smiled.

"Baby!" she exclaimed drunkenly as she looked at the guy and said, "Brendon, this is my girl, Paige."

The guy named Brendon looked at her with confusion and asked, "Girl?" as I smiled and looked at him.

"I'm Paige, Sylvia's girlfriend," I said through clenched teeth as I turned away from Brendon, grabbed Jane and kissed her passionately.

"Wow, that was fucking hot, even for a gay guy!" he exclaimed with a huge smile on his face.

At that moment I felt like a complete fool as Jane laughed and made a fake sad face. She whispered into my ear, "I don't want anyone else. Have a good time" as looked at her with embarrassment.

I turned to walk away from Brendon and Jane but as soon as I turned around there was Marcus. He looked at Jane and looked at me. He looked at me and looked at Jane as a pale and somber look came across his face.

He grabbed me by my hand and pulled me along into his bedroom and locked the door behind him.

"I now know why you're glowing. I thought Jane had the same look to her, but I thought my mind was playing tricks on me. What the fuck is going on?" he asked with concern.

"I don't know what you mean?" I said in a playful and sarcastic tone of voice.

"How long has this been going on?" he asked with growing concern.

"Not that long but it's been building up for a very long time" I replied with happiness.

Marcus placed both his hands on my shoulders and asked, "Have you two lost your minds?"

I slowly shook my head and answered, "We know what we're doing" confidently as he took a seat on his bed.

"Svet can't find out about this," he said with fear.

"There aren't any rules against what Jane, and I are doing," I said as a matter of fact.

"This is not good. This isn't good at all" he said to me. He took a deep breath and said, "Please tell me that you two are just fucking around."

I looked into his concerned eyes and replied, "We are fucking around but I might maybe kind of falling in love with her" as he threw his back onto the bed. He was now laying on his back and looking up at the ceiling.

"Whatever it is you two need to stop it and stop it now. If Svet finds out she's going to be beyond furious."

"Why the fuck would Svet give a shit?!" I exclaimed.

"Are you being serious right now?!" he yelled at me as he sat up in his bed and looked at me as if I had indeed lost my mind.

"Jane is the stallion and you're the unicorn. Do you have any idea how hard it is to perform with a client when you are in love with someone?" he said to me with such passion in his voice it made me take a step back.

"What are you saying?" I asked.

"What am I saying? You just told me that you're falling for Jane and by the look of her I would say you two are in the same boat. Unfortunately, that boat is heading toward a waterfall if this gets back to Svet" he said firmly.

"Marcus, you don't have to worry about us at all. We both know what we're doing. It's your birthday and you have an insane party going on right now. Relax and enjoy your day boy toy" I said with assurance.

He let out a laugh and replied, "Okay...you're right, party on!"

I awoke still drunk with Jane draped across me as she snored loudly into my ear. We were both dressed which was the only reason I knew we didn't fuck around after the party wrapped up.

I lightly tapped her face as she awoke momentarily, smiled at me, rolled over and fell back asleep. I looked at the alarm clock on the nightstand that read 3:11 PM.

I got out of bed, quietly opened the bedroom door and quietly closed it behind me. I walked into the living room to find Marcus, Gina, and Shantel having cocktails.

Shantel looked at me and said, "Good afternoon. I take it that Jane is still knocked out" as I smiled and nodded my head.

"I'm still wasted" I confessed as everyone laughed. Gina said, "Not in a million years would I ever have thought that you and Jane would become an item."

I was stunned! I looked at Gina and asked, "How did you find out?"

"You two making out and groping each other all night long kind of gave it away" she laughed.

"Oh" I replied shaking my head.

"Drink this" Marcus said as I shook my head and replied, "I can't."

"Yeah you can, now drink it, girl," he said as I forced a sip of a Bloody Mary down my throat.

The drink felt like glass going down my throat, but it did make me feel better. I laid down on Marcus' chaise lounge and listened to Marcus, Shantel and Gina crack jokes and laugh.

I remember laying there listening to them when seemingly out of nowhere they all began to cheer, whistle and clap. I sat up as I watched an unable to walk straight, Jane makes her way toward me as she yelled out, "Not so fucking loud! My head is pounding!" as Marcus exclaimed at the top of his lungs, "What?!"

As soon as Jane laid down on the chaise lounge and nuzzled her neck into mine, Shantel said, "Oh, you two look cute together" as Jane said, "Fuck you Shan" laughingly.

"Family oath right now. Whatever was witnessed here stays here including those two" Marcus said out loud.

As we all always did, we all said out loud at the same time, "Family oath."

Later that night Shantel and Gina left together and were heading to Spain together for a client who booked them both at the same time.

Marcus was heading to Canada the following night, so Jane and I headed back to Dallas earlier that afternoon.

The next three weeks Jane and I spent together at my place in Dallas was magical. I had told Marcus that I was maybe falling in love with Jane, but I knew that maybe was no longer part of the equation. I had once thought that I was maybe in love with Danielle, Francesca, and the preacher's wife but what I felt toward Jane was love and so far, above and beyond what I had ever felt before.

I remember getting into my car and going to the supermarket for a few items. When I returned to my apartment, I found Jane sitting on my couch, expressionless and sitting as still as a statue.

When she noticed that I had entered the apartment she smiled at me, rose from the couch and said, "It's time for me to go."

I dropped the grocery bags as I was holding and said, "Why? Why do you have to leave now? We have more time."

"You have more time baby. Svet called me and told me my time is up. I'm heading out shortly and will be on my way to Norwalk to meet with a regular client" she explained to me.

"This isn't fair. She told you had more time. Call her and convince her to give you more time" I said with panic.

"I tried baby, I tried but the answer was no," she said sadly.

We both knew that we both were going to head back to work but we both thought we had more time. I had been trying to mentally prepare myself for that time, but I was ill prepared to deal with it at that specific time. I did my best to try not letting Jane know how upset I was.

"Okay then, I understand. I'll drive you to the airport" I said to her as she smiled and said, "Svet's already made arrangements."

"Who is he?" I asked as she shook her head and replied, "Don't June, just don't."

Less than ten minutes later, we hugged each other, kissed each other goodbye and she was on her way to Connecticut.

I was beyond upset! I thought I could handle her going back to work but the thought of her being touched, kissing someone else and being kissed and her being fucked made me sick to my stomach.

I was pacing around my living room when my work cell phone rang.

"Hi, Svetlana," I said into the phone as she replied, "Hello my darling. You will be going to Paris. You will be picked up in two hours" she said to me.

"I'm still on vacation," I said to her as she laughed and responded, "Vacation time is now over. You seem to be over whatever it was you were going through. It is now time to get back to work."

"Of course," I replied.

It was if I wasn't in control of my own body. I showered, pack my bag and got dressed as if I was being controlled by someone else.

In Paris, I met with a new client. She was young, beautiful and had an amazing body. Marcus had told me how difficult it would be for me to perform but I didn't realize what he was talking about until that night.

I did as best as I could, and it went well. She was happy but for the first time, I felt wrong about what I had done. I felt dirty and disgusted with myself. My mind raced with wonder over what Jane may be feeling. Was she feeling the same way or was it no big deal to her?

Jane and I were being booked constantly. When I asked Jane why she explained that for the time we were both away Svetlana had been losing money and we were playing catch up.

Jane and I talked as much as we could, but it was difficult connecting. It seemed as if we were always in different time zones and in different parts of the country and world at the same time.

As the hours turned into days and the days into weeks I was in a terrible mental state of mind. All I wanted was to be with Jane and I thought of her constantly. I did my best to hide my state when we spoke, but it didn't stop me from hysterically crying after we ended our calls.

It had been a little over three weeks since Jane and I parted ways, but I needed to see her.

I read a text from Jane that read, "I miss you" as I laid in the bed of my hotel room that evening.

"I miss you too. Where are you?" I replied to her text.

"Home. Where are you?" she asked via text.

My experience told me that the likelihood of me being booked before the next weekend was slim so I decided that I would surprise her.

I replied to her text, "In Portland."

She replied with a sad face emoji.

I rented a car and made the bit over two-and-a-half-hour drive from Milwaukee to Jane's apartment in Chicago. It was just past 10 PM when I arrived in Chicago and it took me close to twenty minutes to find a parking space within walking distance to her apartment.

I walked into her lobby and was greeted warmly by the doorman, Gustavo.

"Good evening Ms. Anderson. I'll let Ms. Morozov know you're here" he said to me.

"We haven't seen each other in a while, and I would like to so surprise her. Can you please let me up without calling her?" I asked with a coy smile.

"I don't know Ms. Anderson. I don't want her to be upset with me" he explained.

"I have $200 dollars that say she won't be" I responded with a wink.

He smiled and said, "Go right up and have a great night."

As I exited the elevator and walked to her door my heart was full of excitement and my adrenaline was flowing.

I was about to knock on the door but as I was about to knock, I stopped myself. I instead juggled the doorknob gently to find that her door was unlocked. I smiled to myself and thought that this was going to be a perfect surprise.

I gently turned the doorknob and slowly opened her front door. Her apartment was pitch black. As I entered her apartment my bag accidentally knocked into a potted plant she had. As the plant fell from the small table it rested on I somehow managed to catch it and place it back on the table.

I turned my body, closed the door and as I turned around and took a step forward, I heard "Kiai!"

I was kicked dead center in the chest so hard that I was flung back into the door, knocking my head violently against the door as my body slid down to the floor.

I tried to breathe but the wind had been knocked out of my body.

"You picked the wrong fucking apartment!" I heard Jane yell out as the apartment suddenly became bright with light.

"Oh my God, June! What the fuck?! I thought you were in Portland?!" she screamed out.

As I felt oxygen to fill my lungs, I looked up at her and said, "Surprise."

She dropped to the floor and grabbed a hold of me as she kissed my lips and cheeks over and again.

"I'm so sorry, baby. I didn't mean to hurt you. I'm so sorry, I didn't know it was you, baby" she said with an upset voice.

"It's okay, totally my fault," I said to her as she helped me to my feet.

"Are you okay?" she asked with concern.

"My head hurts" I confessed as she pulled me into the kitchen and wrapped an icepack in a kitchen towel.

"Show me where," she said with tears in her eyes as I pointed to the back of my head and she placed the ice pack wrapped in the towel on the spot.

"I'm so sorry you scared the shit out of me. Gustavo didn't call to tell me I had a guest. I was on my couch reading when I heard the doorknob jiggle. I assumed someone had snuck in and was trying to break into my apartment" she explained to me.

"It's okay, it's my fault. I wanted to surprise you. I didn't expect to get beat up is all" I laughed.

She kissed me and hugged me tightly.

"I missed you so much," she said as I looked at her and smiled.

Jane was, of course, beautiful, but she had a different look to her. Her eyes were a bit puffy and she had light bags under her eyes. The way she looked made me worry.

"Are you okay?" I asked her with concern.

"Yeah, I'm fine" she quickly replied.

"Are you sure?" I asked as she smiled and said, "I've been having a little trouble sleeping is all."

"You've never had trouble sleeping before not ever. I've never met a person who could almost fall asleep so fast. What's going on?" I said to her.

"Nothing is going on, I'm fine," she said to me with a smile.

"Jane don't bullshit me," I said in a firm tone of voice.

"I don't know. I don't feel right anymore. It's like I don't know who I am" she confessed to me with tearful eyes.

"Talk to me," I said to her.

"It's okay, it's just me, it's just…just" she tried to say to me as I took removed the ice pack from my head and placed it in the sink.

I hugged her and kissed her lips gently. "Talk to me Jane, just talk to me," I said to her.

"Working has been hard for me, the hardest it's ever been and it's, it's…" she began to say as if trying to force the words to come out of her mouth.

"Me? Is it hard to work because of me?" I asked with fear.

She looked at me with her tearful eyes and then looked down at the floor as she slowly nodded her head.

"It's been hard for me too" I confessed to her.

She looked up at me and smiled.

"There's nothing you could ever tell me that would change the way I think and feel about you. I want to know anything and everything there is about you" I said to her with assurance.

"Why?" she asked.

I knew what I wanted to say but I was scared that it was too soon. I was fearful that if I said the words that I wanted to say to her she not only wouldn't feel the same, but my words would scare her.

I had regrets in my life, but I didn't want to regret not saying what I felt I wanted to say to her this night. My heart was racing, my palms were sweaty, my head hurt as did my chest, but it felt right.

I gazed into her eyes and said, "Because I love you."

"How can you love me? I'm a fucking whore disaster" she replied with a tear falling from her right eye that ran down her cheek.

"I love you because I love you. I know I do. I've never felt like this about anyone before. I've thought I may have been in love before but now I know I wasn't. I don't know a lot of things, but I do know that I'm in love with you" I said to her with my voice quivering.

Tears were now streaming from both her eyes as she looked at me and said, "I love you too."

I can't describe the feelings and emotions that I felt that night, but I can tell you it was the greatest feeling I had ever experienced. Those four words, I love you too, changed me forever.

We kissed passionately as I pulled her into me. As I began to rub her ass, she placed her hands over mine and pulled them off her.

"What's wrong?" I asked.

"It's not that I don't want to because I more than do. It's just that it's that time of the month and I feel really gross" she said to me with a pained look on her face.

I let out a laugh and said, "I understand, I more than understand. How about we have a few drinks and just talk?" as she smiled and answered, "That would be so great."

She looked at me and asked, "instead of a few drinks how about we do a shit load of shots? I have these amazing bottles of Tequila that I smuggled back home from a trip."

"Sure" I replied with laughter.

What followed was shot after shot of the most amazing Tequila I had ever had.

I felt great sitting there with Jane talking and drinking but I couldn't help but wonder how Jane had learned to kick the way she had kicked me a couple of hours earlier.

"Jane, tell me how you learned to kick the way you kicked me," I said to her.

Her demeanor changed as she looked at me and said, "Let's talk about something else."

I shook my head quickly and said, "I want to know."

She shook her head quickly as I watched tears begin to swell in her eyes.

"Jane, I love you. I just want to know. As I said, there's nothing you could ever tell me that would change the way I think and feel about you."

She gazed into my eyes and said, "My birth name is Brian" which made me laugh hysterically.

"Nice try but all I want to know is how you learned to kick the way you kicked me."

She took three shots of the tequila in succession and then looked at me with glassy eyes.

She sat silent for a moment and then smiled.

She began, "His name was Akihito Yamaguchi and he saved my life. I was fifteen and living on the streets of Chicago selling my body from time to time for a meal and a place to stay for a few nights if I could afford it.

I remember the rain pouring down from the sky. It was late, pitch dark, I was cold and starving. I found an awning to stand under and hoped for the downpour to stop. Thankfully the downpour stopped to a drizzle. As I went to take a step to walk a huge guy looked at me and asked me if I was alright.

I told him I was fine, and I was going to walk home but he insisted that he would walk me. I didn't have a home, so as we walked my mind was flooded with ideas as to how I could get away from him and go about whatever I was going to do that night.

We walked for a few blocks when I found myself walking with this guy on a dim street. As we walked past a storefront there was a small alleyway before the next storefront. As we began to pass, he grabbed me by my hair and pulled me into the alleyway.

He pulled me by my hair a few feet into the alley and pushed me to the ground. He removed a huge knife from his pocket and told me to take my clothes off. I screamed at the top of my lungs for help over and again and he got angry.

He told me if I screamed one more word, he was going to gut me like a fish. He told me that I was so hot that it wouldn't take long so just take my clothes off and let him do what he was going to do.

I was terrified and my entire body was shaking. I rose to my feet as he then told me to drop my pants and panties to my ankles and bend over.

Without hesitation, I did what he said and removed my pants and panties to my ankles. He took me again by my hair and bent me over a garbage can. I heard him unbuckle his belt, unzip his zipped and push his pants down.

I felt his cock rub over my asshole as he held the blade of the knife to my throat. I was so fucking scared. I thought after he was finished, he was going to slit my throat.

He asked me if I was ready to get what was coming to me as I cried hysterically. Out of nowhere, I heard the word "Kiai!"

The blade of the knife was no longer across my throat. I closed my eyes for a moment and when I turned around there was the guy, laying on the ground with his pants around his ankles.

The guy was holding his throat with one hand as he held his balls with his other hand.

There he was, my savior, Akihito.

Akihito walked to me, turned his head to look away from me and pulled my panties and pants back up.

He told me he was going to call the police and I begged him not to. I knew if the police came, I would be taking into custody and put into the foster care system. While I begged and pleaded with Akihito the guy managed to stumble down the alley and run off.

Akihito told me that if I didn't want him to call the police, he would need to call my parents. I wrapped my arms around him and hugged him as tightly as I ever hugged another person in my life. I thanked him over and again.

When he asked for my parents phone number I confessed that I didn't have any and that I was homeless. I continued to thank him but when I tried to walk away, he grabbed my arm.

When he looked at me, I could see the sadness in his eyes. He walked me to a steel door that I hadn't noticed that stood a few feet from where I was almost assaulted.

He took me inside and made me a bowl of white rice and hot tea. He gave me a place to stay, food to eat and clothes on my back without asking for a thing in return. His home and dojo was now my home.

His wife had passed and when she did his business began to die. He barely spoke English and he had students but not many. I was a fifteen-year-old kid and found myself now living with a mid-sixties Japanese Karate teacher.

Akihito Yamaguchi was my savior turned father that I always wanted and never had. He never not once looked at me inappropriately.

I taught him English and he taught me Karate and Japanese.

For the first time in my life, I experienced love. I loved him and he loved me. I was his Musume and he was my Otosan.

He valued education so I earned my general equivalency diploma when I turned eighteen. He didn't have much but he spoiled me rotten. I remember riding the bus with him on our way home from the mall on my birthday.

There was this huge billboard for one of those franchise martial arts places with a pretty woman and handsome guy on it. He looked at the billboard, looked at me and smiled.

He didn't put me on a billboard, but he did take a picture of me in my Karategi. I became the face of the dojo and business began to flood in. The dojo was filled with students and for the first time, he had money.

He was so fucking happy and so was I. Life couldn't have been any better than it was for me. I was so grateful for all he had done for me. He filled a void in my life, and I did the same for him.

Guys in suits started showing up one day it never stopped.

As if out of nowhere, he was again struggling for money no matter how packed the dojo was. I didn't understand why. I tried to talk to him about it, but he wouldn't.

It seemed for as much money was coming in as much was going out. We didn't live any differently, but I knew something was wrong.

Something was wrong, he was paying protection money. The more he made the more they took until he decided he wouldn't pay any longer.

He commanded me to leave but I wouldn't, I knew he was in danger. I felt it in my bones and in my soul.

We fought valiantly but the numbers were against us. When a gun was put to my head he dropped to his knees and said the words, Watashi wa anata o aishite watashi no musume. He said the words I Love you my daughter as I watched fire exit the barrel from a gun and his lifeless body fall to the ground.

I cuddled his lifeless head in my arms as I cried, then darkness, then I met Svetlana."

Jane again took three consecutive shots and then smiled at me.

I was beyond stunned and didn't know what to say to her. I thought for a moment and then said, "Thank you for telling me and I'm so very sorry."

She smiled at me with glassy eyes and nodded her head as my cell phone rang.

I answered my cell phone and heard Svet says the words, "Nashville, tomorrow night."

"Svet, I don't want to go," I said to her as she again said, "Nashville tomorrow night."

"Fine!" I exclaimed as I ended the call.

"Svet booked you," Jane said to me as I nodded my head.

"Fucking shocking," she said with disgust as she looked at me and then said, "Come lay down with me."

It wasn't that I didn't enjoy laying in bed with Jane that night as she rubbed my head and twirled my hair. I just felt that something was wrong. After what she had told me about her life, I didn't want to ask her anything more. After all, we had nothing but time on our hands.

I went to Nashville and met with my steady Christian singer client. I hadn't seen her in quite some time, and she knew almost immediately that something was off with me.

I had only been there for a little over an hour and we were having cocktails when she looked at me and asked, "Are you okay?"

"Of course. Why are you asking?" I asked.

She looked at me with concerned eyes and smiled.

I let out a laugh that couldn't hide my feelings as she looked at me with a sad look present on her face.

"What do you want to do tonight. Start with a massage and take it from there?" I asked as she shook her head and replied, "Tonight I just want to enjoy a few drinks and your company."

"Seriously?" I asked with surprise.

I looked at her beautiful face and said, "I'm confused."

She smiled and stroked my face. She took hold of my hand and walked me into the all too familiar room with the bar in it. She made a couple of drinks and slid one across to me from behind the bar.

She took a sip of her drink and said, "Tonight I'm saying goodbye to you."

"Did I do something wrong?" I asked with panic filling my being.

"No, quite the opposite. When we first me I was so confused over who I was, but that confusion is gone forever, and I have you to thank. Thank you for everything you've done for me" she said with pride.

"This is it? This is the last time I'll ever see?" I asked.

"I'm retiring. I'm going to get sued by the record label and take a huge financial hit, but I can't live like this anymore" she said.

"You're coming out publicly?" I asked with a stunned tone.

"No, not publicly but as I said I can't do this anymore. I'm selling the house and leaving the country. I've met someone and we're going to be together" she said with a smile.

"Who is she?" I asked with anticipation.

"To the world, no one in particular. To me, she's the most important person in the world" she said with happiness.

The most important person in the world? She was giving up everything she had for a special someone. She was giving up what she loved more than anything to be with her. At that moment all I could do was picture, Jane.

"That's so romantic," I said as I began to cry.

She again touched my face but this time from across the bar.

"I knew something was off. You're in love, aren't you?" she asked with a smile.

I took a sip of my drink, nodded my head and replied, "That I am."

"Who is she?" she squealed with a high-pitched tone.

"To the world, no one in particular. To me, she's the most important person in the world" I said, repeating the very words she had said to me only a few minutes earlier.

She let out a laugh and said, "Just do what I'm doing. Leave the life you now live behind and be with her."

"I don't know if it's that simple" I explained as she looked at me and responded, "It can be if you want it to."

I spent the night with her but for the first time ever nothing sexual happened. We drank and spoke all night long. When it was time for me to leave, we hugged each other tightly, thanked one another and said goodbye for the last time.

I knew I would be seeing Jane at Svetlana's in a few days and I was over the moon with excitement. My mind was made up. I was going to tell Jane that I wanted us both to stop being working girls so we could be together.

Svetlana greeted me warmly as did Sergei at the door when I arrived.

"Welcome home my dear," she said to me as I kissed her on the cheek and made my way to the backyard where Gina, Marcus, Esmeralda, and Javier were having drinks, laughing and catching up. As everyone else arrived I eagerly waited for Jane to arrive. It wasn't unusual for her to be the last to arrive but tonight felt way off.

The sun had already set when Jane walked into the backyard wearing a pair of sunglasses. I remember thinking how odd it was that she was wearing sunglasses although the sun had set.

Before she could make her way to us, Sergei stepped in front of her and walked her back into the house. I remember feeling anxious.

I stared at the time on my cell phone and watched the minutes pass by. It had been close to an hour already and I was becoming worried.

Svetlana appeared from inside of the house and called me to her by waving her index finger at me. I walked over to her and smiled but my smile was not returned.

"Come, my dear," she said to me as I followed her into the house, up the long winding staircase, and to a bedroom door.

"You talk to her now," she said as I looked at her with confusion. Svet opened the bedroom door as I stepped inside. Once inside, she closed the door behind me.

The worry I felt left my body as soon as I saw Jane. I ran to her and kissed her lips as she kissed me back and held onto me tightly.

"What the hell? Take those sunglasses off" I said to her as she slowly removed her sunglasses.

She looked terrible! She two black eye's and her bottom lower lip was split in the corner.

"I've missed you so much," she said to me with tears in her eyes. The worry that had left my body was now back with a vengeance.

"Me too," I said to her as she began to cry.

"Don't cry," I said to her as I embraced her tightly.

"I messed up bad," she said as my worry now turned to fear.

"What happened?" I asked.

"Things have bee so hard for me. I knew I wasn't performing up to standards, but I pushed forward. Svet already talked to me about it and she wasn't happy. I was warned to get my act together, but I messed up, I really messed up last night."

"What happened?!" I exclaimed.

"I met with a new client last night and I tried my best, I really tried my best, but I just couldn't. While we were in the act, I tried my best not to, but I started to cry. Once I started to cry, I couldn't stop myself. He became angry and then irate. He stopped fucking me and punched me in the middle of my face. I got dressed and left" she explained through sobs.

"Listen, we don't have to do this anymore. We can just leave and be together. I don't want to ever see you this way again. I love you Jane and I want to be with you, always" I said as I too began to cry.

"I love you too!" she cried out as she gently kissed my lips and held onto me as tightly as she ever had before.

"Just tell me you want to leave this all behind us. We don't have to do this anymore. We have more money then we can spend in a lifetime" I said with hope.

"June?!" she cried out.

"What?!" I responded.

"You can't be serious right now?" she said with a stunned tone.

"I'm as serious as a heart attack. Come on, we're leaving" I said with conviction.

"Oh my God! You are serious! No way, there's no way you can be this naïve!" she screamed out.

What the fuck was she talking about? I may not be the sharpest knife in the drawer but I'm not naïve I said to myself silently.

"June, please tell me you're joking right now," she said to me.

"I told you I'm dead serious!" I yelled out.

"Who in the fuck do you think we work for?" she asked.

"Svetlana!" I yelled back.

"Who is Svetlana?" she asked.

"Our fucking boss!" I replied.

"No shit!" she exclaimed as she rubbed her face with both her hands.

"June, who do you think she is?" Jane asked me with concern.

"I told you our boss" I replied without thought.

She took a deep breath and said to me, "Baby, yes Svetlana is our boss. She's also Bratva. How could you not know this?" she said to me with angst.

"What in the hell is Bratva?" I asked.

Jane wrapped her arms around me and gazed into my eyes. "Baby, Bratva is the Russian mafia."

"Russian mafia?" I asked incredulously.

"June, how do you think this is all possible? We get paid five figures to meet with clients every time. We meet with the wealthy, the powerful, the famous, and confidentiality is guaranteed. Did you ever think how this is all possible?" she said with her voice quivering.

I shook my head quickly over and again with disbelief.

"You said when it's time, you would leave and live in Thailand. We can do that right now, together" I said with hope.

"It's time when Svetlana says it's time. My time is up baby" she said through sobs.

"Bullshit! We can leave whenever the fuck we want. She doesn't own us!" I screamed out as Jane cried out, "Yeah, she does own us."

She placed her hand under my chin and forced me to look at her.

"We are all her property. Each and everyone one of us has something in common. None of us have family or close friends other than our own little dysfunctional family of ours. If any of us disappeared, who would notice? Who would care? Who?" she asked.

No! This couldn't be true! There was no way this could be true!

"No way! I'm going to talk to Svet and get all this bullshit squared away right now!" I exclaimed.

"No! No! No! Don't! Please don't!" Jane cried out.

"Svet will understand!" I screamed out.

She grabbed me, kissed my lips gently and said, "I'm so sorry."

As we gazed into each other's eyes she sobbed and said, "I told you at the start that this could only end badly. I knew it but not only did I let it happen it happened because of me. I know what's going to happen, but I need you to know if I could take it all back I wouldn't. You've made me so fucking happy. I didn't know what happiness was until we became involved. I didn't remember what love was until we became involved. I now know what life should be, but it's too late. Thank you for loving me and making me so fucking happy. My only regret is that what happened between us didn't happen sooner. You're going to live a long and happy life and all I ask is that when you think of me you think of me fondly. When my time comes, I'll smile at the thought of you and embrace the darkness. Without you, there is no light."

"What are you saying?" I cried out.

"As I said, my time is up," she said while nodding her head.

Suddenly, the bedroom door flung open. I swung my body around as Sergei walked in. He grabbed me violently by my hair. As he dragged me out of the bedroom by my hair which was wrapped in his hand, he looked at Jane and said, "You are not to move" as three men I had never seen before entered to the room.

I knew where he was leading me. It was a room I was all too familiar with. It was Svetlana's office, a place where we drank, spoke for hours and where I felt connected to her.

He opened the door, pushed me inside by my hair and slammed the door behind me.

Svetlana looked at me with a look I had never seen before.

"Sit, my dear unicorn," she said to me as I nervously took a seat in front of her desk.

Svet looked angry and gazed at me so cold that it made me shiver for a moment.

I looked at her defiantly and said, "I want out."

"Why would you want such a thing?" she asked.

"I love Jane, she loves me, and we want to be together" I replied.

"I know but It's not that simple" she replied.

"I don't understand why it can't be? Neither of us would ever say a word. We would just go away and live happily" I said forcing a smile to appear on my face.

"Jane is already going way. What would also go away is your earnings and that cannot be allowed. A stallion may be replaced but a unicorn may never" she said stoically.

"What do you mean by Jane is already gone?" I asked trembling.

She smiled and coldly replied, "What does one do with a thoroughbred when it is no longer a thoroughbred? For example, a racehorse that can no longer race?"

"You could put it out to pasture" I replied.

She smiled and replied, "Or you put it out of commission permanently."

"No, please no. I'll do anything. I'll replace her" I begged.

"My dear, you cannot replace her. You are my unicorn for a reason and one reason only. If it were that simple I would do it, but it is not" she replied.

"Please, all I want is to be for Jane and me to be free!" I cried out.

"If you would like to be free, I may grant that if you wish" she responded as I nodded my head.

Svetlana yelled out something in Russian which led to Sergei entering the room. He again grabbed me by my hair, pulled me from my seat, and pushed me down to the floor.

"Do you wish to be free my unicorn?" she asked.

I want to say something, anything but I'm terrified that I may say the wrong thing.

All I wanted was to be happy and to live my life but as I look up from my knees, I don't think that either is possible.

She again says something in Russian but what happens next, I can never have never imagined. Sergei pulls a gun from his waist and presses it hard in the middle of my forehead!

"Do you wish to be free?" Svetlana asks as I cry and beg, "Yes, but I don't want to die. Please don't kill me! I thought we were friends. I thought you were the mother I never had. How can you do this to me? Why would you do this to me? I love you and you're asking me if I want to die? All I want is to be with the person I love and who loves me. We're all supposed to be a family."

I'm going to die! I don't want to die! If I could start things anew I would except for Jane. My mind is flooded with thoughts and memories of my life. I'm going to die but at least I finally feel what it's like to truly be in love.

I close my eyes and await my death as I can think of only Jane.

As we all hear screaming, yelling and gunshots come from outside her office door. Svetlana says something to Sergei in Russian. I don't understand the Russian language at all, but I can tell from the tone of her voice she's worried and afraid.

 Sergei removes the gun from the middle of my forehead and looks at Svetlana.

I can't stop my body from trembling. What just happened? Is Jane okay?!

Sergei puts the gun in his waistband, walks to the door and opens it.

I watch from my knees as Sergei's body falls backward and crashes to the floor with the word "Kiai!" yelled out from Jane's voice.

Jane is bleeding from her cheek and is limping a bit as she removes the gun from Sergei's waistband.

She looks at me and smiles and then becomes fixated on Svetlana.

"This is all a farce. This supposed fucking family of mine and yours isn't a fucking family at all. It's your way of control. How are you mom?" she asks.

"My stallion please," Svetlana says as Jane raises the gun and points it directly at Svetlana.

"You don't give a shit about any of us! We're just dollar signs to you!!" she screams out as she punches the gun in Svet's direction.

Jane screams out at the top of her lungs and then begins to laugh. I know Jane won't hurt me, but I'm scared! I don't know what is happening!

"Baby get up," Jane says to me with a smile as I somehow manage to rise to my feet with my legs trembling.

Jane scratches the side of her head with Sergei's gun and laughs.

She fixates on Svetlana and asks me, "What happened in here?"

"She told me she would set me free and Sergei put his gun in the middle of my forehead," I say through sobs.

"Did she?" Jane says out loud as she smiles at Svetlana and walks over to Sergei who is still laying on the floor unconscious.

She places the gun in the middle of Sergei's forehead and laughs. She looks at Svetlana and asks, "How does it feel mom?"

Svetlana jumps up from her seat and screams out, "No! Please!"

"Not so nice when the shoe is on the other foot," Jane says with conviction.

"Sit the fuck down bitch!" Jane commands as Svetlana sits down in her chair.

"You're not my mom. My mom was a strung-out bitch, but she's was my mom. You, on the other hand, fucked my head up so bad that for a long time I thought you loved us, me especially. I've always been your stallion and my baby here has been your unicorn for quite some time. Tell me the truth, you've never loved any of us!" she exclaims.

"That is not true! I love you all!" Svetlana screams out.

"Liar!" Jane screams out in response.

"It is not my choice. I have no choice" Svetlana says as she begins to cry.

"I had a choice once. Join my father as in be set free or work and live life. Kind of fucked up wouldn't you say, mom?" Jane asks sarcastically with the gun still pointed in the middle of Sergei's forehead.

"No, please, don't hurt him!" Svetlana screams out.

As Sergei begins to regain consciousness Jane smiles and knocks him out again with a perfectly placed heel kick knocking him out again.

"That client last night wasn't a client at all. He was going to kill me, and you knew he was. You didn't warn me, didn't say a fucking word. Why? Because you know I'm in love with June and I won't be able to do what the fuck I've been doing for the last six fucking years?"

"It was not my decision! It was out of my hands! The order came from above!" Svet exclaims.

Jane looks at me and asks, "Would you like a drink?"

I look at her as if she's has lost her mind and reply, "I don't feel like drinking right now."

Jane laughs and replies, "You have to try this. The most magnificent Russian vodka you'll ever taste. I insist."

"If you insist, then okay" I reply.

Jane walks to the liquor cabinet in Svetlana's office, opens the door, grabs a bottle and three shot glasses

She pours three shots, hands me one and slides once across the desk to Svetlana.

"Cheers whore!" she exclaims as she once again points the gun to Svetlana's head and smiles.

Svetlana downs the shot as Jane smiles at me and we drink our shots.

"That was so smooth!" I yell out as Jane blows a kiss at me, smiles and replies, "Told you so."

"I want more!" I yell out. It's not that I really want it but after I drank that shot, I calmed down and I want to calm down even more.

Jane has me take a seat across from Svetlana. She pours me another shot and places the bottle in front of me. I drink the shot, another, another, another and I now feel beyond calm.

"Really June?" Jane asks comically as I reply, "Really Jane."

I look at her and say, "There were three guys in the bedroom when Sergei pulled me out by my hair. How?"

"Even with two black eyes and a busted lip, I'm still hot. A look, a smile, a little boob and they were all mine" she answers me.

"What the fuck did you do?!" I exclaim with anger.

Jane rolls her eyes and answers, "Beat their asses. They're all tied up in a compromising position" with a laugh.

Jane looks at Svetlana and smiles as she places the gun on the desk.

"The order came from above but again, no warning, no nothing from you. After all these years it's good to know that I mean so fucking little to you that you would allow me to die. Better yet, isn't what those three men in the bedroom were supposed to do? Hmm, Svet?" she asks.

Svetlana looks at Jane and replies, "Da."

"You were going to have me killed in your own home. Do you have any idea how this makes me feel?" she asks with her voice wavering.

Tears stream from Svetlana's eyes as she looks at Jane and says, "It's is not my choice."

Jane laughs in a manner that makes me nervous as she again takes the gun and points it at Svetlana.

"Call him, call him now!" Jane screams at the top of her lungs.

"I cannot do that!" Svetlana cries out.

"You have two choices Svet, make the call or be set free. You have five seconds!" Jane says in such a cold voice that it brings a shiver to my body.

"Jane, no, please don't, please don't" I cry out.

"Goodbye, Svet!" Jane yells out as Svetlana grabs her cell phone.

"I will call," Svet says through sobs.

"On speaker!" Jane yells out.

"Hello," a male voice says with a thick and heavy Russian accent.

"Hi, Nikko," Jane says out loudly.

"Who is this?" Nikko replies.

"It's Sylvia, Nikko. It's been a long time" she says.

"Privet simpatyashka. How have you been?" he says with a genuine tone of joy.

"I'm not going to lie. I've been better. Svetlana and I are having a discussion and I'm hoping you can provide insight. I was booked yesterday and the client I met with tried to kill me. I show up for Svet's super awesome party and again three guys were going to kill me. Svet told me that the order came from above and since you're the top of the pyramid I want to hear it from you. Did you order Svetlana to kill me?" she asks.

"Net. I do not do such things. I am businessman. Old business was done that way, not now" Nikko explains to her.

"So, it would be safe to say that Svetlana was doing things on her own?" Jane asks Nikko.

Nikko replies, "I'm very upset now simpatyashka. You have my word, Svetlana will be accountable for such actions."

"Thank you, Nikko but I have another thing to ask of you," she says with tears in her eyes.

"Da chto eto?" he asks.

"June and I don't want to do this anymore. We want out. May we please leave?" she asks.

"It is not quite that simple. You and June bring in lots of money very good for business. You two leaving no good for business" he replies.

Jane closes her eyes tightly as I watch tears stream from her eyes. She opens her eyes, take a deep breath and slowly exhales.

"Let's talk business then. How much Nikko? How much for June and I to be free?" she asks with her voice cracking.

The silence is deafening.

"$5 million U.S." he finally replies.

I look at Jane with sadness and begin to cry.

"Nikko, Svetlana tried to kill me twice. Had she succeeded my earnings wouldn't matter. Please, I beg of you" she cries out.

"$3 million U.S. I feel it is a very reasonable price. Don't you agree?" Nikko replies.

"Thank you so much, Nikko. $3 million U.S. is more than reasonable. I'm grateful for your understanding" she says as she smiles with a mischievous look at Svetlana.

Jane sits on the desk directly in front of Svetlana and presses the gun into her forehead.

"Nikko, Svetlana feels bad about trying to kill me and all and she would like to make the payment to you on our behalf. Isn't that right Svetlana?" Jane says as she pushes the gun so far into Svetlana's forehead, she pushes her head back.

"Svetlana, $3 million for the girls and $2 million for your actions. Wire tomorrow. That is all" Nikko says as he ends the call.

Jane removes the gun from Svetlana's forehead, spins herself around on the desk and slides herself over to me.

"Nikko will not be happy when I tell him I agreed to pay only because you had a gun to my head!" she screams out.

"Maybe, maybe not but you did agree. Besides, if you're telling me you're not going to pay then why should you still be breathing?" Jane says with anger.

"After all, I have done for you this is the way you repay me. I saved your life!" Svetlana screams out.

"You took my life from me and you tried to kill me twice since then. What the fuck exactly is it that you did for me anyway? You paid me to get fucked, over and again while brainwashing me and everyone else for years! When something happened that I wouldn't have imagined in a million years, as in me falling in love, it's not allowed. Fuck Svetlana, you made more money from my pussy then I did. So, what exactly did you fucking do for me?!" Jane yells out.

I rise from my seat and pull Jane off the desk by her legs. I kiss her and slowly take the gun from her hand.

"We're free, let's go," I say to her.

"You two will never be free! I will find you and when I do it is over for you both!" Svetlana yells out at the top of her lungs.

"Stand up bitch!" Jane commands as Svetlana rises from her seat, stands up and walks out from behind her desk.

"Kiai!" Jane screams out as she kicks Svetlana in the face with a roundhouse kick, knocking Svetlana to the floor.

Jane gets on top of her and begins to pummel Svetlana's face, over and again, alternating between left- and right-hand strikes.

"Stop, Jane, please stop!" I scream out as I tug and pull on Jane from behind to try and stop her from beating Svetlana to death until she finally relents.

"We need to go now!" I yell out as Jane gains her composure. As Sergei begins to awaken Jane sites on top of him says, "Bye Sergei" and knocks him out yet again with a perfectly placed strike to his face.

"What now?" I cry out to Jane.

"Now we leave," she said to me.

"What about the others?" I asked her filled with emotion.

"Forget about them. It's just me and you know" she replies to me.

"But they are, our family" I cry out.

"No, June. They're not our family. Forget about them. They need to find they're own way" she says to me.

"But Marcus. Marcus is my friend" I cry out in pain.

"I know but it's much easier to stay under the radar with just me and you. Marcus will be fine, trust me" she said.

"Where are we going to go?" I ask with fear.

"I don't know but I do know we need to get out of here now" she commands.

As we left the house and walk down the front stairs, I look out to the backyard to see all the people that were such a big part of my life. None had a clue as to what had happened since Sergei removed me from the party and brought me into the house.

Jane and I exit the house through the front door and get into Jane's rental car. As she drives away from the house, I turn my body and watch the house disappear from my sight not knowing what the future holds.

We drive for hours and leave the state of California and enter Nevada.

"I'm exhausted. We should get a room for the night" Jane says to me with tired eyes" as I nod my head in agreement.

We find a cheap motel and get a room for the night.

As soon as we enter Jane throws herself onto the bed and looks at me.

"We need to close our bank accounts," she says to me.

"Okay," I reply.

Closing my bank accounts was not hard at all. I never moved my money from my bank in Nevada but Jane closing her accounts posed a challenge. We had to get to Chicago. The bank she had her money with only operated in Chicago.

The next morning, I walked into a branch, closed my account and walked out with every penny to my name in cash that I placed in a small suitcase I purchased a few stores down from the bank.

We then began our trip to Chicago. Close to 30-hours later we arrived in Old Town, Chicago. As I drove past Jane's apartment, she noticed a black sedan, with tinted windows so dark you couldn't see inside.

"Fuck!" she screams out.

"What?" I ask with fear.

"We can't get into my apartment. Just drive us to the bank so I can get this done" she said to me.

I drove her to the bank as just as I had done a couple of days earlier, Jane cashed out her bank accounts.

We both sat in the car not knowing what to do or where to go from here.

"We need to leave the country," I say to her.

"It's not that simple baby. I don't have my passport and I can't get into my apartment to get it. Even if I could and you had your passport we can't travel under our real names. It'll be too easy for us to be found" she explained to me.

"Is Svetlana really going to try and find us?" I ask her with terror.

"Yeah, she is and if she does, we're fucked," she says to me as she places her hand on my cheek.

"Isn't there anything we can do? Are we supposed to just live our lives looking over our shoulders every minute of the day? This is no way to live?" I cry out full of fear and emotion.

"I don't know baby. I need time to think" she replies to me.

"Maybe we should head to your cabin," I say to her as Jane shakes her head and replies, "Svetlana knows about the cabin. We would be sitting ducks."

My entire body is now shaking, and my eyes are becoming full of tears.

"I need you to calm down, okay?" Jane says to me as I can't stop the tears from flowing.

"I'll try" I reply as Jane looks at me and says, "I'll drive, switch with me."

As Jane begins to drive, I feel hopeless and full of anxiety. I climb into the back seat, close my eyes and cry myself to sleep in the fetal position.

I don't know how long I had been sleeping but as I open my eyes, I sit up in the back seat to read a sign that reads Welcome to North Dakota.

"We're going into North Dakota?" I ask Jane with surprise.

"Yeah" she replies to me.

"You're from North Dakota?" I ask her with a stunned tone of voice.

"No, I was born and raised in Nebraska," she says as a matter of fact.

"I'm confused. Why are we in North Dakota?" I ask her.

"I think my dad lives here" she replies.

"You're dad? I thought you didn't know your dad" I ask her with shock.

"I don't know my dad but I'm pretty sure he's been looking for me" she replies.

"He's been looking for you?" I ask her as she pulls the car over on a long stretch of road.

She turns the car off, exits the car and takes a seat on the hood as I exit the back of the car and join her.

Jane grabs her cell phone, scrolls through the phone and hands her cell phone to me.

I look at the screen of the cell phone and lock my eyes on the screen.

"Missing, Amanda Nyman, age 1, last seen June 11, 1994" I read.

"Whose Amanda Nyman?" I ask.

"I think I am" she replies.

"What? Why would you think that this little girl is you?" I ask with intrigue.

Jane goes into her purse, opens her wallet and hands me a tattered picture that is held together with Scotch tape.

I look at the picture she had just handed me and look at the image on the missing child picture. I flip the tattered picture around and read Jane's 1st Birthday.

"I'm sorry, I should have asked you first, but I need to know. I need to find out why my life turned out the way it has. I don't know how this is all going to turn out for us, but I at least need to know if I have a family" she explains to me.

"It's fine. Where are we going?" I ask her.

"I have an address and the name of who I think my dad is. That's where we're going" she says to me.

"When did you find this out?" I ask her.

"Eight months ago. I was on FaceBook and an advertisement for a missing kid website popped up with what I think is my baby picture, the same picture your holding in your hand. I called the number and inquired. Long story short I was given the name of Bryan Nyman was told that he was in North Dakota. I did an online search and found a website for an insurance broker named Bryan Nyman" she explains to me.

She takes her cell phone from my hands, scrolls again and hands me the phone back. I look at the screen and gaze at a picture of a handsome man who appears to be somewhere in his early to mid-forties. His eyes look so familiar.

"You have his eyes!" I exclaim as she nods her head in agreement and smiles.

"I think so," she says with a smile.

"Alright then, let's go," I say to her with conviction as I hug her tightly and give her a kiss on her cheek.

We get back into the car and drive for a while until we arrive at a decent size home with a manicured loan. Jane turns the car off and looks at me.

"Here goes nothing," she says as she gets out of the car as do I.

There's a minivan parked in the driveway that we pass by as we make our way to the front door of the house. The door is open behind a screen door. Jane rings the doorbell as we wait for someone to answer.

A few seconds later a pretty woman, probably in her late thirties comes to the door holding a cup of coffee.

She looks at us both and asks, "Can I help you?"

"I don't know if you can but I'm looking for Bryan Nyman" Jane replies.

"Who might you be?" the woman asks.

"My name is Jane" she replies as the woman gets a pale look to her and drops the cup of coffee to the ground.

"Please, come in," she says to us as she unlocks the screen door and lets us both in.

She walks us into the living room and asks us both to take a seat on the couch. I look at one of the end tables to see the same picture that Jane has, the same picture on the missing child poster, sitting in a frame.

"Why are you looking for Bryan?" the woman asks.

Jane looks at the woman and replies, "I think he might be my dad."

The woman cups her hands and places her cupped hands over her mouth.

"Why would you think that?" she asks as I hand the woman Jane's tattered picture.

"I'm Bryan's wife, Donna," the woman says as two kids, a boy, and a girl enter the living room.

"Kids go outside to the backyard and play," Donna says as the boy replies, "Mom I'm thirteen. I don't play in the backyard. I'm going back to my room to play PlayStation" as the girl smiles and replies, "Okay, mommy."

Donna looks at us and says, "Those are our kids. Paul is 13 and Courtney is 9."

Donna looks at me and asks, "You are?"

"I'm sorry, I'm June, Jane's girlfriend" I reply with a smile.

"Girlfriend as in girl who is a friend?" Donna asks as Jane looks at Donna and replies, "No, she's my girlfriend."

"Oh, okay, great. Will you two excuse me for a moment?" she asks us as I reply, "Sure."

As Donna exits the living room, she grabs a cordless phone on her way to the kitchen and returns a few minutes later.

"Can I get you two anything?" she asks as we both shake our heads.

"I called Bryan. He's on his way here from his office. He shouldn't be too long" Donna says to us.

Donna takes a seat in a small chair across from us as we all sit in awkward silence for what seems like forever.

Suddenly, we here the screeching of car tires just outside, the engine of a car turning off and a car door open and slam shut.

The screen door flies open as a tall handsome man, the same man that Jane had shown me a picture of earlier comes running into the living room.

He takes one look at Jane and says, "No way, it can't be, A.J.?"

Jane slowly rises to her feet and becomes fixated on Bryan.

"A.J.?" she asks.

Bryan smiles and replies, "Amanda Juliet" as Jane repeats, "Amanda Juliet?" and he nods his head.

"How old are you?" he asks as Jane replies, "I'm twenty-five" as he smiles.

"What's your birthday?" he asks.

"April 25th, 1993" she replies.

"What's your mother's name?" he asks.

"Abigail" she replies.

"That was actually her middle name. Her name was Suzanne Abigail" he replies.

"Was?" Jane asks.

"Yeah, was, she passed away a long while back" he replies.

"Drug overdose I assume," Jane says as Bryan nods his head and replies, "Yeah."

"Do you know what happened to her husband?" Jane asks.

"He was killed by the father of a little girl he molested before Suzanne passed. Had to be about nine years ago by now" he replies.

"Karma," Jane says out loud.

"May I ask you something?" Bryans asks Jane.

"Of course, what is it?" Jane asks in response.

"My daughter had a birthmark on her upper right arm. May I see your arm, please?" he asks her.

Jane raises the sleeve of her tee shirt, exposing the birthmark I knew was present on her arm.

As I look at Bryan, I see a tear fall from his left eye and roll down his cheek.

"May I hug you?" he asks her as she nods her head.

When they embrace, she puts her head on his shoulder and begins to cry as he rubs her back.

She pulls away from him and smiles.

"It was nice to meet you," she says as she looks at me and says, "Let's go."

"Go? You just got here. Where are you going?" he asks with concern.

"I'm not sure but I need to go" she replies.

"No, you can't leave. We have too much catching up to do. You need to meet your brother and sister. You need to meet your grandparents, your aunts and uncle" he says with panic.

"I have a family?" she asks filled with emotion.

"A huge family, A.J. You can't leave, you're home now," he says with tears now streaming from his eyes.

"What happened to your face?" he asks with concern.

"Had a little altercation is all but I'm fine" she responds.

Bryan looks at Donna and smiles.

"Sweetheart, can you get the guest room ready?" he asks with his voice quivering as Donna nods her head and replies, "Of course, honey."

He looks at me and says, "You must be June. It's so nice to meet you" as I smile and reply, "Likewise."

Bryan takes hold of Jane's hand and says to me, "Will you please excuse us for a moment?" as I nod my head and he walks her out of the living room and into the backyard.

A moment was over three hours long as I sat in the living room with Donna and Jane's stepsister Courtney.

When Bryan and Jane appeared again in the living room, they both looked as if they had been crying. Both of their eyes were bloodshot red.

Donna prepared dinner, we ate in the dining room and called it a night a few hours later as Jane and I entered the guest room.

"I don't think we should stay here. If we're in danger so is everyone we encounter" Jane says to me with concern.

"What do you want to do?" I ask her.

"I think we should take off first thing in the morning" she replies.

"Is this what you really want?" I ask her with concern.

"No, but it's the right thing to do" she replies as she begins to cry.

"What did you two talk about?" I ask her as she cuddles against me and looks into my eyes.

"Everything. I told him everything" she says to me.

"How did he take it?" I ask as she replies, "He feels responsible."

That night Jane told me that her dad was taking her mom to court for sole custody when she took off without a trace. How her dad immediately went to the police and filed kidnapping charges against her mom and report her missing. That her dad went so far as to get age enhancement photos of her made to no avail. That although he did his best to hope for the best, he feared that she would never be found. That now that she found him and knew she had a family she felt closure. That if our lives ended tomorrow, she could die knowing that at least someone other than me loved her and wanted her.

In the morning I awake first and make my way from the bedroom to the living room where Bryan sits on the couch reading a newspaper, sipping a cup of coffee with a national news program playing on the television.

He smiles at me and asks, "Did you sleep well?" as I nod my head and smile.

A few minutes later Jane joins us. As soon as she enters the living room Bryan jumps off the couch, hugs her and kisses her on her cheek.

"Good morning A.J.," he says as she smiles and replies, "Good morning."

"Big day today. We're having a welcome home party for you. Everyone is coming, your grandparents, aunts, uncles and cousins" he says to her as she looks at me with a dumbfounded look.

"I need to head to the office for a little and pick up a few things for the party, but I'll be back soon," Bryan says as he again kisses her on the cheek and heads out of the house.

"I don't know what to do?" she says to me as I shrug my shoulders and confess, "I don't either."

On screen, the words, "Malibu Massacre" appear on the television as Jane and I lock eyes and then become fixated on the television screen as video plays of Svetlana's house in flames appears.

There are fire trucks, firemen and police in the background as the reporter stands in front of yellow police tape with the camera rolling.

"Malibu residents are in a state of shock this morning as the home behind me exploded in flames a little past 11 PM last night. Once the fire department was able to get the fire under control, extinguish the flames and enter the home, five bodies were found inside, bound, gagged, shot execution style and burned badly. Foul play is suspected as an accelerant was used to start the fire in what appears to be an effort to hide the gruesome scene inside.

What we do know is that the home is owned by businesswoman Svetlana Orlov and her husband Sergei Orlov. They are co-owners of a successful corporate recruitment firm in downtown Los Angeles but as if this moment none of the remains have been identified" the reporter states as Svetlana's neighbors are interviewed.

After a few interviews the reporter ends the segment by saying, "As I said, residents are stunned and shocked at the events of last night. We'll bring you further news once more details become available. For NNT this is Rodger Dowling."

Jane and I sat in stunned silence for a while as we looked at each other until her cell phone rang. She answered the call and put the cell phone on speaker.

"Nichego ne govori i zhivi zhizn'yu. Vy dvoye svobodny" was all the man's voice said before the call was ended.

"What did he say?" I ask Jane with terror.

"He said to say nothing and live life. You two are free" she says with tears streaming from her eyes.

"Who was that?" I ask as she shakes her head and replies, "I don't know."

As I stare at A.J.'s face as she licks my pussy from in between my legs this morning with drowsy eyes it sometimes feels as if my life was some sort of movie script. It sometimes doesn't feel real.

However, I know this feels real as my body explodes with pleasure as I have an Earth-shattering orgasm. I could wake up like this for the rest of my life I think to myself as A.J. removes her face from my pussy and kisses up my body and to my lips.

"Good morning baby," she says with a smile as I smile and say, "Good morning love" as we kiss.

"I'm going to take a quick shower and open up for the day. Are you coming?" she asks as I smile and reply, "Yeah, I need to get a few things from the supermarket, but I'll be by in a couple of hours."

"Great," she says as she kisses me again, gets off, the bed and heads into the bathroom.

As I lay in my bed with a feeling of pure joy running through my body and soul, I know that I couldn't be any happier.

It was once A.J.'s dream to live out her life in Thailand but she's now living her dream here with me and her family in North Dakota.

I can't believe it's been three years since she received the phone call on her cell phone. We were both nervous and concerned for a while but as time passed, I think we both came to the realization that we didn't have to live like that anymore.

We purchase a small home a few blocks from A.J.'s dad and purchased a small building a few miles from our home where she opened "Yamaguchi's Dojo." She's been training me since she opened and I'm coming along. Karate is a great workout and I enjoy it.

The dojo doesn't make a lot of money but there's more to life than money. I know this now. I've lived the life of excess yet have never been happier. Money was once intoxicating to me and I couldn't get enough of it. I realize now how foolish I was.

A.J.'s love is more intoxicating to me than any amount of money can ever be. The love we both receive from her family is priceless to me. I often wonder if my dad would be proud of me had he known what I had become and what I now was. I know that some questions will forever be asked but can never be answered like what happened to the people that I once referred to as my family?

I once worked in an ice cream shop. I once worked as a waitress, a masseuse and then owned and operated my own massage business. I was once a high-end escort and now work as a receptionist and trainer at my girlfriend's dojo. A working girl I'll always be but I will never go back to lead the life I once did.

Printed in Great Britain
by Amazon